Pharaoh

A Novel of Ancient Egypt and the Slave Queen

William Burr

This is a work of fiction. Names, characters, businesses, organizations, places, events and incidents either are the product of the author's imagination or are used fictitiously. Any resemblance to actual persons, living or dead, events, or locales is entirely coincidental.

Pharaoh

ISBN-13:978-1535355032

ISBN-10:1535355034

Station or power does not define love

Contents

Pharaoh

A Novel of Ancient Egypt and the Slave Queen

William Burr

Forward

Ancient Egypt, a civilization in Northeastern Africa, was concentrated along the Nile River, the world's longest, a river that flowed from deep in the interior to the Mediterranean where silt piled up for eons creating a lush, fertile delta. On this great delta and at the edge of the sea, Alexander the Great, built a city called Alexandria.

While much of the rest of the world languished in the dark, Egypt flourished. Over its four thousand years of history, pharaohs and kings were at the center of knowledge and riches, rule passing from one pharaoh to the next, living gods who ruled with absolute power.

In this rich city of Alexandria, a library containing 700,000 scrolls brought learned men from all over to study, conduct scientific research, publish, lecture on the world's learning. Today's university is the closet organization that resembled the Mouseion.

But there were other similarities to our lives today, Cities dominated. A structured business environment supported by government gave great wealth to the few. Religion was a strong influence on all Egyptians. Learning and education were prized possessions. Women were often educated, allowed to own property, and listened to by the men. Children were raised with great care and love. Much of the way we live in the 21st century was almost identical to life in Ancient Egypt.

Yet there were numerous differences compared with today. Pharaoh's and Kings ruled as gods. The after-life was believed to be more important than life on earth. With a multi-theistic religion, people worshiped dozens of gods often choosing one as their personal favorite. Wars were almost constant. Slavery was common. Men often had multiple wives as polygamy came and went over the ages. Unlike our conservative western morality of today, nakedness or near-nakedness was fashionable especially with slaves who wore almost nothing, their masters wearing provocative clothing and elaborate jewelry and cosmetics.

Into this environment, came Akhu and Sabra

Chapter One - The Mouseion

Though frowned on by the studying scholars, Akhu chased his sister, Sabra, through the halls of the Mouseion, raising the glances of learned men and illustrious visitors who read scrolls at low tables in the massive library.

"You will never catch me," shouted Sabra running as fast as her wraparound skirt allowed.

"By Osiris, I will. No girl can outrun a boy."

Rounding the corner of a Moorish, tiled wall, he peeked ahead. Sabra was nowhere in sight. He looked everywhere, along the large complex of buildings, then out among the gardens surrounded by richly decorated lecture and banquet halls that were linked by porticos and colonnaded walks.

Where did that girl go? he thought looking up and down the portico.

A few scholars passed, nodded familiarly, and walked on, talking quietly about a Greek philosopher named Socrates.

She stepped out from behind a Greek statue, hands on her hips, a huge smile on her lovely face.

"Who's the smart one in this family?" she asked with a grin.

Akhu drew a deep breath then turned when he heard his name called.

"We're coming," he shouted to their governess, Rania. "Quickly, it's time for the evening meal."

Taking his sister's hand, he led her out of the courtyard that was flanked on both sides by other buildings and a massive library. Living there, they were not impressed by the structure housing most of the worlds knowledge, scroll after scroll assembled with enormous care and visited by learned men from the far corners of the earth. The Mouseion of Alexandria was governed by their father, Hepu, a powerful position and appointed by the Egyptian king, Nebrunef.

The children followed Rania, hand in hand but a dozen feet behind her as their station demanded. No public connection with a commoner was allowed.

"She is so bossy," Sabra said.

"Shh. She will hear you and punish me with more of that awful Greek writing."

"You're almost as smart as she is," Sabra laughed poking him in the ribs.

"Behave. That is not proper in public," Akhu said in a voice that cracked, evidence of the changes coming rapidly, changes he didn't fully understand.

Rania held the curtain aside and ushered the children into the inner courtyard of their home, a noble's residence. They walked toward a table set at the far end in the shade of an olive tree.

A maid brought two bowls as the children sat.

"Your mother wishes you to be ready for your dance lesson," Rania said to Sabra. "And you, young man, will do an hour of Greek for that comment."

Akhu gave Sabra a look wondering why he was being punished for what she had said.

Finishing, Sabra stood just as her mother came down the outside staircase and over to her daughter.

""How many times must you be told not to play in the library? It is not for children. Your father will be angry and will see that you are punished. Now, get into your dance toga. The teacher will arrive within minutes."

"Yes, mother," Sabra said racing up the stairs to the children's room.

"Son, you will tell your father and accept his punishment."

"Yes, mother," Akhu said, his head down, damp eyes looking at his sandaled feet.

She looked at him, her favorite child, the one so much the future depended on. But, where was he headed? So far he'd shown no exceptional skills though he mastered everything that he was taught. Nekbet was a stern mother, stern but fair, she thought. How else would she rise in this world? Certainly not as the wife of Hepu who would never become more than the head librarian of Egypt.

She looked again at Akhu and gave him a rare smile.

"Go with the archer and practice."

"Yes, mother." Akhu said and left with his head still bowed, fully aware that his father's punishment would be severe.

Akhu was called to the room in the Mouseion where his father spent much of his time. Hepu, a man of considerable weight and girth, sat on a pillow, Moroccan style, eating his evening meal with his fingers. A young woman brought Akhu into the room and waited in the background as the boy stood, head lowered, eyes on the floor, in front of his father.

"Again it has happened," Hepu said as he licked his fingers and nodded to the young woman.

She immediately brought a tumbler of beer and poured into his cup. Akhu stood quietly and waited as he drank.

"Your punishment for disobeying would be severe if it were not for other matters of greater importance."

Akhu looked up at his father's worried expression.

What is wrong, father?"

The old man shook his head and drank more from his cup.

"You are too young for such matters."

"But, how will I ever learn anything if I am always too young?"

A small smile crossed the man's face then died away.

"I am afraid bad times are upon us, my son. You are right. It may be wise for you to know what is about to happen."

His father sat up and leaned forward, the ample skin under his chin hanging down like a small sack.

"You mother and sister should not worry as this is between us. Is that clear?"

"Of course, Father."

"One of the scholars has told us that the Sea People have attacked Pelusium, a day's ride by camel from here."

"The Sea People?"

"They are vicious plunderers of anything of value, uneducated, warriors from birth, and too close to us for comfort."

"What can be done to prevent them from coming to Alexandria?"

"Very little. It is said that King Nebrunef is on his barge on the sacred river. He is more interested in the construction of his tomb than the danger that awaits in Pelusium."

His father took the boy's hand and pressed it to his lips.

"They will come here. It is only a matter of time. You will leave Alexandria and take your mother and sister to the Upper Kingdom. They will think it a lovely escape from the heat of summer."

"But, Father?"

"How often must you be told to obey? Take them and go. Take them to Aswan. You must guard them with your life."

Akhu stood on the dock, his young body straining under the weight of chest armor and a sword hanging from his waist whose tip scraped the ground as he walked.

A servant girl helped his mother onto the boat, holding her arm so she wouldn't fall as the boat rocked on the small waves of the Nile. Sabra held Akhu's free hand, smiling, a laugh on her lips, carefree and happy at the thought of a long trip up the Nile to the first cataract and the ancient city of Aswan.

The women sat on an open bench under an awning. But, Akhu, hiding the real reason for their journey, stood at the rail looking back at Alexandria as the oarsmen moved them away from the dock and into the current. His thoughts went to his father and what would happen when the Sea People came to his beloved city.

"Isn't this wonderful," Sabra said coming to him by the rail

She took his hand again and squeezed.

"We can swim in the river, play in the olive groves, and there will be no need to study. So, why do you look so sad? Does being with me all the time make you unhappy?"

"I hate leaving father alone in the city."

She laughed and gave her brother a kiss on the cheek.

"Always trying to be a man, are you? " she said pushing at his sword. "Such a boy and dressed like a soldier. Well, let me tell you. I am able to take care of myself. I don't need any help from you and that silly sword that you probably can't even swing above your waist. Play soldier if you like but let me remind you, I am better at the games than you are or ever will be."

He smiled at his brave sister, a year older than he was, and already a beautiful woman who would soon be given to some man to make the family richer and more important, something his mother never ceased talking about.

How he loved this wonderful sister of his. They had always thought they were naturally born from his mother and father but had recently learned that Sabra was the daughter of one of their father's slave women who died in childbirth. Filled with guilt, Hepu had told his wife that they would raise Sabra as if she were their daughter.

His thoughts were interrupted by Sabra poking his ribs with her fingers, teasing him as always.

"And how are you, a mere girl, going to protect us?" Akhu asked with a grin.

"Like this," gripping his hand tight, sweeping it over her head, spinning around, then bending over, and pulling Akhu to the ground.

On his back, he looked up at her, eyes wide, yet pleased in some way.

"Where did you learn such a thing?"

"I don't only study women's things. Rania has shown me much, some things you obviously don't know."

She offered her hand to help him up but he grabbed her arm and pulled her down on top of him.

"You see," he whispered in her ear, "Never think you have won."

He kissed her neck. She smiled and kissed him on the lips, a long leisurely kiss that did strange things to his young mind.

Chapter Two - Slavery

The boat was an hour out of Alexandria, the rowers straining against the spring current of the Nile, a muddy, heavy flow of life-giving water to this country of desert. Akhu stood at the rail, his arm around his sister's shoulders, pointing out a camel train plodding upriver on the bank.

"Mistress Nekbet!" the young maid shouted to their mother, then screamed.

Both Akhu and Sabra spun around. Upriver and heading toward them were four boats loaded with armed soldiers, a blue and white flag flying from each.

"The Sea People," Akhu whispered as he unsheathed his sword.

Sabra looked at him, back at the onrushing boats, over to her frightened mother, then back at Akhu.

"Your sword will not save us from twenty soldiers. Put it away. If we don't fight, they may leave us alone."

Understanding the truth in her words, Akhu sheathed his sword and moved to the bow where he could see them better.

The enemy swept down until two of boats banged onto opposite sides of theirs, the other attackers turning and pointing upstream into the current to stand by if they were needed.

Ten men jumped on board, their leader pointing to the luggage bags holding their possessions. Satisfied there was no resistance, he walked up to Akhu.

"Hand me your sword." the man said in a rough voice.

Sabra nodded that he should do as asked. Realizing she was right, Akhu unbuckled it and gave it to the soldier.

"What do we have here," the man said looking under the awning at Nekbet and the young maid, the girl holding their weeping mother. "Take them."

Nekbet screamed when the men came closer, beat against them with her fists when grabbed around the waist and lifted up. Each were held in the attacker's arms like two sacks of grain.

While his mother and the girl were roughly dragged off the boat and onto the invader's craft, Akhu stood to his full height and said, "No. You will not take them.."

The leader raised his hand and brought it down hard on Akhu's neck dropping him to the deck. Sabra fell to her knees and took his head in her hands, the front of her linen dress hanging open showing youthful breasts that brought laughter from the other soldiers.

"Bring them," he said stepping over Akhu and picking up the boy's sword.

Held in a desert camp east of Alexandria, Akhu, Sabra, his mother, Nekbet, and the maid knew nothing of what was happening. He was grateful that they were allowed to be with each other yet wondered why they were kept separate from the other prisoners he had seen when they arrived. Time stood still as they were fed in the darkness of what appeared to be a storage shed, no windows, only a wood door through which they sometimes heard voices.

That is, until one day when a man came into their hovel, took Sabra by the arm and dragged her out of the dark, bug infested shed.

"Akhu! Akhu! Don't let them take me from you," she screamed.

He ran after her but was bludgeoned to the floor by a guard.

Ten minutes later, he woke in his mother's arms.

"The man said he is coming for you next. Be strong, my son. Sobek, the crocodile God will protect you."

"I will not leave you."

"The maid and I are done for. But, you must grow, learn, watch, look for the smart thing to do. Try to help your sister. Be the great man I know you will be."

"But, mother, what will become of you?

She smiled and patted his arm, the closest to affection he'd ever felt from her.

The door slammed opened and three men came into the room. One dragged a struggling Akhu to his feet and out the narrow door. The other two reached for his mother and the maid. As he was led away, their screams rocked the still, night air.

His shoulders ached and his fingers bled but none of the slaves were allowed to rest. His pickaxe swung up and then down as hard as he could against the rock, chips of sandstone flying when it struck, razor sharp shards that cut into his legs that bled as profusely as his palms.

Another boy who worked beside him, stopped to wipe the sweat from his brow. Before he could raise his axe again, the flat of a sword hit the back of his neck and dropped him to the ground.

Akhu turned to face an overseer, a black man twice his size, standing over the fallen boy with a wide grin on his face. Without a moment's hesitation, and before the guard could react, Akhu's axe came down and buried deep into the black man's chest.

Silence fell over the group. Akhu stood over the bleeding body and screamed.

"No more. I will take it no more."

The other slaves looked dumbfounded and frightened at what this strange boy had done. For a moment, Akhu thought they might join him but, twenty soldiers arrived on the run and the slaves retreated back to cutting stones for the king's tomb.

Akhu was knocked to the ground and dragged to the tent of one of the Sea People's leaders.

In a language he didn't understand, the soldiers told the man what happened. They were dismissed and Akhu stood in front of a soldier who looked like he had been in a hundred battles. Scars were on his face, arms, and legs. One eye was missing, a jagged hole in its place.

"Who do you think you are by defying your masters?" the man said from where he sat on a pillow.

"My friend was beaten for taking a moment to wipe his brow."

"Do you not yet realize you are a slave?"

"It is made clear every moment of every day."

"So, why do you fight? Why do you not accept your fate?"

"This is not what I was raised to be."

"And what is that, pray tell?"

"I am a scholar, a learned person not a cutter of stone."

The man smiled and leaned back.

"Do you read?"

"Yes, Greek and Egyptian, some Persian."

"How old are you?"

"I will be fifteen years in a month."

"Can you read this?" the soldier said handing him a scroll.

Akhu unrolled the papyrus and smoothed it out with great ceremony like he had seen scholars do in the library of Alexandria

"It is a calendar, a telling of the days of the year."

"What use is such a thing?"

"It tells when the moon is high and full. It tells when the spring birds will arrive in Egypt. It tells much you must know to be a good leader."

The man stroked the tufts of beard hanging from his chin.

"You will move into my tent and teach me things."

Akhu smiled.

"I no longer have to cut stone?"

The man came over and gripped the boys bicep.

"You have become as strong as one of my soldiers. Now, is the time to use your mind and be of help to my people."

It was difficult to tell who was the teacher and who was the pupil in the days and months that followed. Justin, or One Eye, as Akhu called him, sat for as many hours that the soldier could keep his eyes open learning to read. His people had no need for an education, boys being raised from the cradle to fight, girls to serve them. But One Eye had bigger plans. He wanted more than living in a dirty tent in some far away land nursing the wounds of battle. He had seen farms in the north and great cities along the delta but his life had always been nothing more than an expendable soldier. In young Akhu, he had found a possible solution.

For Akhu, the protection of One Eye was his salvation. He'd quickly understood that the soldier was his way out of the stone mines and the lowest form of slavery, one that cared little whether he lived or died. With the protection of One Eye, a respected leader of a large group of the invading Sea People, he would at least survive. His mother's last words rang in his ears. "Learn, watch for your opportunity."

One Eye was merciless in his training of Akhu. Twice a day, One Eye had the boy face an experienced soldier who sparred with him until he could no longer raise his sword off the ground. Hours were spent running in the blistering heat to toughen his growing body. At night, by the camp fires, Akhu was challenged by one, sometimes two soldiers, to a wrestling match, grim entertainment for the bloodthirsty warriors. Fortunately, wrestling was something Akhu was good at and he won more often than not.

Slowly, Akhu and One Eye formed a bond, first of mutual respect, then one that grew into something akin to friendship.

It happened one hot afternoon. Their unit of Sea People had sailed east past Judea to the shores of Assyria. Their attack on a rich city thrust One Eye's group into a fierce battle with seasoned Assyrian palace guards. He and Akhu had been forced against a wall, fighting back to back against overwhelming odds. Both were covered with cuts and slashes.

Akhu, realizing the tight spot they were in, took a second to look up and see a hanging awning overhead. Quickly, he reached and pulled it down onto the heads of their attackers. The two of them slashed into the struggling mass of men, killing them all.

"Well done, my little friend," One Eye said. "You may make it after all."

The months turned into a year as One Eye, Akhu at his side, roamed the lands of Africa, fighting, robbing his victims of anything of value, and moving on. It was the way of the Sea People. They had no interest in conquest only in sacking and burning for their profit.

That is all but One Eye. With his newfound knowledge, taught by Akhu, his dream was one of a land his people could settle in and prosper.

Slowly, One Eye and his successes in battle, came to the attention of his superiors. He rose in rank until he sat by the side of Mattu, the Sea People's king. Akhu, though seated behind, was always allowed in the great man's presence.

"If what you say is true, Egypt will fall when Alexandria is taken," Old Mattu said to One Eye.

"I have learned much from the Egyptian boy. He is a good fighter but will not fight against his people. I would ask your mercy and allow him to stay behind when we attack?"

The king turned to look at the young man, a strapping youth of obvious Egyptian heritage.

"You are taking the word of this young man that their king is weak and nearly powerless."

"He has not said so but it must be assumed that King Nebrunef is weak. All he wants is stone for his tomb that he buys from our mines at exorbitant prices. His armies are weakened without a strong leader. I believe the time is right. Overpower their king and Egypt will fall. Finally, the Sea People will have a home."

Mattu looked at his favorite general and smiled.

"You have ambitions that should worry me?" the king said.

"I only think of my people as all should do."

Chapter Three - A Merchant Slave

Sabra sat in the dark on the floor of the one room, adobe house, her arm around the maid. Her mother lay at her feet, arms tied behind her back, legs splayed out with blood coming from between them. She had not made a sound for the last hour making Sabra more afraid than she'd ever been in her life.

She had been spared what her mother and the maid had been through, repeated rapes by the Sea People's soldiers. Why, she wondered? Maybe I'm too young for them? But, the maid is young too. My poor mother. She looks more dead than alive.

Laughing came from bored guards outside the hut, men who had been given the lowly job of keeping the women locked up and away from the common soldiers.

"Are you all right, Nina?" Sabra whispered to the maid.

"I hurt but I will be all right, Miss. We must get out of here or our fate will be the same as your mother's"

"How? There are guards at the door."

"Come. Follow me."

Nina led her by the hand toward the back of the single room house and ran her hands ran along the dark wall until she found what she had seen while on the bed pad below, a wood window, sealed with dry mud so no light would come in.

Quietly, the two girls dug at the mortar and pried it open with their fingers. Nina gave Sabra a boost onto the sill then held her breath for fear of the noise as the girl dropped to the ground outside. Agile as a cat, Nina clawed her way up and out to join Sabra where both froze like statues, listening, wondering what to do next.

A bolt of lightning fell from the sky announcing a coming storm, a moments light in the dark night.

"This way," Sabra said taking Nina's bleeding fingers in hers.

They made their way down a narrow alley and out onto a deserted, cobbled street. Sabra made a quick decision and hustled them away from the river toward the desert that began within sight of where they stood.

"No, Miss. We should not go there," Nina said.

"To go anywhere else is to meet more rape and death. We must go where there are no men."

Nina followed her into the night.

Light was forming in the east as the two girls stumbled up one more dune of sand.

"I am too tired," Nina said. "Can we not stop?"

"We must find water before the heat of the sun kills us."

At the top of the dune, they looked down and saw a small oasis, two scraggly date palms growing out of some scrub grass.

"There. I told you. Where there are trees there will be water."

"But, look?"

Coming from the opposite direction, plodding through the sand, was a small caravan of camels and donkeys destined for the same oasis. Men walked beside camels, each holding a lead and urging them toward water.

On the back of each beast. a huddled bundle swayed back and forth that soon became obvious were people covered in robes.

"Nina, we have two choices. Go and meet them and ask for help or stay here and die from the afternoon sun."

"There are men among them."

"And probably families as well. We will ask for protection and it will be given."

As the caravan neared the oasis, the girls staggered and slipped down the side of the dune and walked toward a man holding the lead camel.

"We are in need of water just as you are," Sabra said. "And would request the protection of your caravan."

The man, his face burned by years in the sun, a scar on his cheek and small eyes that darted back and forth, spoke in poor Egyptian.

"What are two young girls doing out in the desert alone?"

"We got separated from our caravan. Please help us."

The man looked them up and down and smiled.

"Of course. Help yourselves to water then join us by our fire. We will talk."

Sabra smiled at Nina, took her hand, and led her to the small pool of water. When they had finished drinking and bathing their faces, they stood and walked toward where the leader sat by his fire. Food would be there.

The maid pointed to a huddled group of figures under a tree, all covered with robes and bound hand and foot.

They came toward a circle of men around the fire. In the center two young men stood wearing only breech cloths, men who looked like those she had seen wrestlers wear at the games in Alexandria.

"Sit," one of the wrestlers ordered.

The girls sat in the sand as the two men faced each other, squared off, and began a ferocious fight. The one who had ordered them to sit, threw the other to the sand almost immediately. Both tumbled over and over, hitting each other with closed fists, scratching, biting, drawing blood.

The girls sat, hands to their mouths, not knowing what was happening. The man who had spoken sat on the other wrestler's chest, his hand around the fallen one's throat and squeezed. As they watched, the loser's eyes went wide then closed and his whole body relaxed.

The winner stood, grabbed the maid by the hand and led her away. Sabra screamed startling the camels who snorted and moved restlessly on their hobbled feet.

The leader came over to where she stood.

"She is of no value. But you will join our group and be taken with the others to the market."

The sale was swift. Sabra was sold to a man wearing city clothes, a man holding a child's hand.

"Your owner is Yusef," the slave auctioneer said, " He has paid a handsome price. Obey and you will find peace."

She stood in her soiled, white linen dress, eyes darting in every direction, a frightened expression on her young face that told of confusion and fear.

"Come," the man said. "We have a long ride ahead of us."

The child, a boy of around five or six, stared at her from behind his father. Still clutching his father's hand, he looked around at her, his eyes wide at all he had just witnessed.

"Take the child and guard him with your life," the man said giving the boy's hand to her.

She took it and gave the child a weak smile, the best she could do under the circumstances. Sabra knew all too well what was in store for her. Though little more than a child herself, she was fully aware that slave girls of her age were given to a man, none of which involved the girl's desires. As she walked behind the man, holding the young boy's hand, she wondered if that was why she had been purchased.

Slavery in Egypt was common, most often for male workers in the fields or female servants in a wealthy families home. But this man, Yusef, had said, "Take the child and guard him with your life." Maybe she shouldn't be so worried? Maybe she was just meant to be his Amma, his caretaker and not the man's woman?

They rode all day, finally coming to a small town.

The man stopped at the entrance to a gate, knocked, and was admitted by an overweight man with a child's face. He looked like eunuch's Sabra had seen in Alexandria, men who had been made like women and she was sure when she heard his high voice.

"Follow me," he instructed Sabra as the father took the boy inside an adobe house at the far end of a long courtyard.

"You will reside with the others, a bed pad, a jug of water," the eunuch said walking ahead through the courtyard and pointing. "The latrine is behind that building. Old Yuma will instruct you. Listen and obey her and all will be well."

The woman called, Yuma, stood in the open entrance of a small, adobe building at the side of the courtyard that the eunuch he had pointed to. A quick glance showed an outdoor kitchen on the opposite side of the yard. Neither were shaded like the main house at the other end that had a number of leafy trees overhead.

Inside, the heat was stiffling and the smell terrible. Yuma said nothing just pointed to a bed pad in a dark corner among a number of others. Girls slept on some. Others were empty.

The woman came to her with two, white linen dresses in her hand, held them up to Sabra's soiled dress, and handed her the smaller of the two.

"Put this on and come to the kitchen," she said in a voice that cracked.

After the woman left, Sabra looked around, went to her assigned area, and pulled off her old dress. A girl, two bed pads away, giggled. Ignoring the girl, she turned her back and dropped the new dress over her shoulders, ran her hands over the sides to smooth it down on her hips then stepped into a pair of papyrus reed sandals she found at the foot of her pad.

As she left the room, she wondered why the girl had laughed. Sabra was a developed as any girl and had been told so by her maid. Maybe it was the sight of her baggy underpants, maybe it was... Oh, what's the difference, she thought? I'm a nobody here. No one knows about Alexandria and my home at the Mouseion, no one.

In the kitchen, a young man knelt fanning an open fire with a dried papyrus leaf. Two girls peeled tubers. Another stirred a pot of bubbling grain. Yuma stood with her arms crossed giving occasional directions then turned when Sabra arrived.

"You will take these plates of dates to the table and serve them. Do not speak. Do not look at them. Put the plates down and come back for the next course."

Sabra nodded and picked up two plates mounded with dark, sweet dates and went in the direction Yuma pointed.

Entering through a wide entrance that led into the main house, she stepped into a large room, cool and with a fragrant smell. A bowl of incense smoked in the corner.

Seated at a long table was the man, Yusef. At the opposite end sat the young boy. A small, dark skinned woman starred at Sabra from her seat on the side.

"This is the new girl. Do you approve?" he asked the woman.

She looked up from her bowl and stared long and hard, then motioned for Sabra to come closer. Holding the two plates of dates in her hands, Sabra walked over to the woman being careful not to spill.

"She is lovely," the woman said in an Upper Nile accent. "Was she expensive?"

"No, a steal. Will she do?"

The woman smiled and touched Sabra's arm.

"She is soft and, from what I see, unlearned. Yes, she will do very well."

The young boy grinned as Sabra handed him his plate of dates.

She barely slept that night wondering what would become of her. Her mother had been raped to death. Her maid had been taken away by some awful wrestler who killed another man to have her. Now, she'd been sold to this merchant, Yusef, who had told her to be his son's protector. How would she ever get back to her father? How would she deal with this new life she'd been thrust into? She was somewhere on the Nile above Alexandria but not as far as the Upper Kingdom. There was nothing around but desert. May be she was near Aswan where she'd once gone with her father and where they were headed when attacked? She'd ask one of the other serving girls then shuddered at what her young mind thought might happen.

At dawn, the girls rose one by one, stretched, pulled on their dresses, and wandered out to the latrine. The girl who'd laughed, one of the older ones, sat on her pad and smiled at Sabra.

"It looks like you've been chosen and you've only been here a day. I don't get it. You have tiny breasts and are just a young girl?"

"I'm to be the boy's caretaker," Sabra said.

The older girl laughed and shook her head.

"Is that what they told you?"

"Of, course. Why would they lie?"

"Because, the master needs the number one wife's approval before he takes you to his bed, that's why."

"But..."

"Be happy about it. Fight it and you'll be sent to the market again and face far worse. He's not so bad."

"I've never..."

The girl smiled, got up, pulled her dress over a full, woman 's body, and left the sleeping room.

What was that awful girl saying, Sabra thought as she stood and dressed? Her time had come months ago but she was an aristocrat's daughter, a girl who would be matched with a boy who would bring advantages to their family not to be ruined by some merchant on the edges of the Nile. The girl couldn't be right.

The young boy's name was Nino, a bright child but weakened by some strange disease that made his hands and feet gnarled and almost useless. She'd noticed when they walked from the slave market how he'd limped but now saw how bad it was.

"You must do things for me," Nino said as they sat on a stone bench in the courtyard.

She looked at his deformed hands and smiled.

"Why don't I teach you how to hold a pen?"

"I cannot. I have tried many times."

She picked up a quill and wrapped a piece of cloth round and round the stem until it was fat as a chicken leg.

"Try to hold it this way," she said bending his fingers around it and squeezing them tight.

He held it up, stared at the funny looking writing instrument, and smiled.

Together, they dipped it into ink and wrote on a piece of papyrus until he was able to do it himself.

She looked up and saw the father staring down at them.

"Come with me," Yuma said handing Sabra a thin, linen dress, new and clean.

She pulled it on and followed Yuma out into the night, along the stone path and into the main house. The man of the house and his first wife stood in the light of an open fireplace, flames silhouetting them.

Yuma brought her close and let go of her arm.

"You decide," he said to his wife. "Tonight will she be yours or mine?"

The woman smiled, took Sabra's hand and gave it to her husband.

"Tonight she is yours."

Chapter Four - The Sea People

The Sea People's King, Mattu, afraid of the ambitions of his general, One Eye, but needing him, decided to make a thrust east again, a second attempt to sack Beirut. Two years earlier, he'd made a massive attack from the sea and was soundly beaten by troops of the Vizier.

This time, he decided to make a two pronged assault, one by sea with his strongest force, and another by land led by General One Eye.

With Akhu at his side, One Eye embarked from his camp on the east bank of the Nile for a long march through the Levant to the distant city of Beirut. It was his plan to live off the land as they tramped through the mostly unpopulated countryside and avoid constant battles along the sea coast where there were nothing but enemies.

For three weeks they struggled through hostile desert with little water or food. Five thousand men suffered yet plunged on with the dream of vast riches blinding their agony.

Finally, the army mounted a hillside and looked down on the huge city. Minarets soared into the sky with cries to prayer echoing across the valley. Cooking smoke rose tantalizing the hungry. Cattle roamed a far hillside.

At sea, from their elevated place, they saw the fleet of the Sea People waiting for his signal.

"What do you think, my friend," One Eye asked Akhu.

"I think it is a very big city with many warriors. We must surprise them. Nothing else will win for us."

"I agree. We will attack at midnight. Send a runner to signal the fleet."

At exactly the hour of twelve, five thousand soldiers swept into the sleeping city as another ten thousand landed from the sea. Swiftly, they obliterated the four military outposts at the corners of the city and moved ruthlessly toward the center where great riches lay in wait.

For two days, the Sea People sacked the city, raping, pillaging, drinking, stealing, burning, until ancient Beirut lay in ruins.

"This is wrong, One Eye, and you know it," Akhu said as they drank wine in a small cafe by the water, a cowering native girl serving them.

"Wrong? What can be wrong about taking a city like this. We have never done as well before."

"It is wrong to kill in order to succeed. I really believe we should win the hearts of people who will then follow you and there will be no need for killing. It is what Alexander did and look what he created?"

"Ha!" laughed One Eye taking a huge gulp of his wine. "What is the sport in that?"

"Killing is not sport. It is wrong. Look at all the people who have died over these last two days, ours and those of the enemy? What if we still had them? Think of it? All those talents would be alive to make this place even better than it was. Now it is in ruins."

One Eye looked at him and smiled at his young friend.

"You are a dreamer but you also have good dreams. If it were only so."

"We can make it so if it is your wish."

But, this was not to be. King Mattu had other plans.

Chapter Five - The Rabbi

The merchant's wife left her husband, Yusef, with Sabra, giving the girl a kiss on the cheek, smiling, then leaving them alone in the room.

"You please her greatly and that makes me happy. Come. Remove that gown and sit beside me," Yusef said reaching out for her.

Sabra's eyes darted around the room, a closed window, the door she'd been through led by the wife, a bed, a chair, and the merchant leering at her.

He sat on the edge of the bed, hands reaching out, a huge smile on his face.

All her life, Sabra had heard stories from the maids and older girls about what to expect from a man but she really knew next to nothing. Her mother had always told her to obey adults, that a woman must do certain things to earn the security of a man but what she knew was only that of a young girl, bits and pieces of knowing.

"Come," he said in an deeper voice. "Remove my robe."

She stepped forward. He put his hands on her hips as she reached around and undid the clasp holding his toga. It fell to the bed exposing a naked man, the first she had ever laid eyes on. Her hand went to her mouth and she let out a little cry.

He reached up, his fingers at the V of her dress and began to slowly pull. She tried to move back but his other hand held her close.

A scream from below made his head snap toward the open window. Quickly, he let go and jumped up, ran to the opening, and looked down into the courtyard.

A dozen men rushed through the gate. Yuma was the first to fall from a sword thrust to her stomach then two other servants were killed. Orders were shouted by a man dressed in black standing in the entrance. More men rushed up the steps, one stabbing the merchant's wife, then pulling a jeweled necklace from her throat. Another chopped off two of her fingers and removed garnet rings.

Sabra, the top of her dress torn, cowered in the corner as men rushed into the bedroom. With two strokes they dropped the merchant who rapidly bled out from a severed arm. Ignoring him, they stared at her trembling against the wall.

"Here is another," a man shouted to those below.

He grabbed Sabra by the arm and dragged her down the steps to the courtyard. where four other girls were being held captive.

The man in black walked in front of them, nodding in a half-interested way until he came to Sabra.

He stared into her angry eyes, looked at her young body, and smiled.

"How dare you treat me like this. I am a woman of Alexandria," she shouted defiantly.

The man roared with laughter.

"A woman, indeed. Look at you, nothing but a child."

Sabra spit at the man who grinned as his head dodged to the side.

"You are a feisty one," he said taking her arm. "Child or not, you will come with me."

He dragged her off toward the entrance with Sabra clutching at the torn top of her dress.

Outside the gate, she was thrown up and onto the back of a waiting camel and a cloth wrapped around her head. Sabra could see nothing, only hear the clop, clop, clop of the camel's swift feet as it plodded off into the desert.

Hours later, tired and sore from the long, uncomfortable ride, the camel stopped and Sabra felt it kneel in the sand. Suddenly, the cloth was ripped away. She blinked in the bright sunlight but saw she was in front of a wealthy looking person's home, an adobe building of two stories with wide windows open to a breeze off a river that had to be the Nile. Surrounding the house and across a courtyard, was a tan, adobe wall higher than a man could reach.

A guard took her by the arm and led her into the cool interior of the home. Floors were covered with rugs from far off lands. A tapestry hung on a far wall. Pillows lay in clusters facing a gurgling, fountain of water. Mosaic tiles in geometric shapes covered the walls. From an opening in the ceiling, water poured over the edge and fell like rain into a small pool below. It was like something she could only have dreamed of back in Alexandria.

The man in black sat on a pile of pillows as two young girls fed him dates and bread from a porcelain plate.

"Sit," he said pointing to a pillow nearby.

A guard stood at the door. The two girls looked at her with what she felt was sympathy and backed out of the room.

"Sit, I said."

Frightened, she lowered herself onto the pillows and tucked her feet under herself, something her mother had taught her long ago.

"Tell me more about your Alexandria," he said putting another date into his mouth.

She looked more carefully at him, tall, muscular, black hair tied in a knot behind, bright black eyes that never stopped moving, and shiny white teeth that all but glowed when he spoke. A very pretty man if he wasn't so gruff and demanding, she thought.

"What is it you wish to know? I have no secrets."

"Do you read and write like I hear many do in your city?"

"Yes. Egyptian, Greek and some Persian."

"And are all citizens as well educated?"

"No, only those who come from royal families and their servants."

"Were you a servant or a royal?"

"My father is the head of the Alexandria Mouseion, a marvelous place."

"I have heard of it. In fact, I have studied from some of the copies of texts that are in your library."

She smiled wondering why the questions about her old home?

"You seem perplexed," he said. "Are you surprised that a man who kills also reads?"

"I know very little of these things. As you said, I am just a young woman."

He smiled showing those beautiful teeth and nodded his head.

"Bring her some dates and grapes," he called to the young girls who waited in the shadows. "We have much to talk about."

For the next hour, he asked a hundred questions which she answered in the best way she could. Then, his face clouded over and he leaned forward.

"Tell me about your god?"

"Which god? We have many, at least thirty or more. My favorite and the one my mother prays to is Isis, the fertility and mother goddess., the sister-wife of Osiris and the mother of Horus."

"The sister-wife. Do you mean she married her brother?"

"Yes, it is common in Egypt especially among the royal family."

"We do not do that. It is taboo."

"Why?"

"You breed a horse too close and he will be weak and dumb."

"There are many in the royal family like your horses. May I ask who is your god?"

"I am a Jew. We believe in One God and pray to him. It is written that a savior will be born one day who will come to save the world and convert all the non-believers."

"Do you really believe that? One god who can do all things? It is preposterous. Who will look after the crops in the fields as Hathor does, the goddess who gave birth to all life and nourished it through her milk? Who will make the children be born alive like Isis does? Who will protect the King like Osiris does and ward off Seth, the god of evil and darkness? My father worships Seshat, the goddess of libraries and literature."

"My one God does all that and more."

"I can see we have little to speak about. Our lives are very different."

He leaned back on his pillow, his eyes roaming up and down this bright and beautiful young girl, her body bursting with youth and energy.

"I have enjoyed this conversation. It isn't often I get to have an intelligent talk with anyone out here in the far desert."

"Even if we disagree?"

"Even if we disagree, I have enjoyed this. You will be made welcome in my home, a room of your own, a servant to care for your needs, and a full stomach."

Her mind reeled at what was happening. She was in the home of a very rich, man who believed as the Judeans did, a man who had slaves, who gave orders to men who killed and raped, yet who was kind to her and educated.

"Why are you doing this? I am nothing but a slave to you."

"Ah, but you will become more as time passes. You will see."

As young as she was, she understood the implications of his remarks and the look that glistened in his black eyes.

Chapter Six - One Eye

Another year passed and Akhu became the leader of thirty soldiers, all hand-picked men who were assigned as One Eye's personal guard. Not every one of the Sea People's invasions had been successful. Some had failed but the army of One Eye stood out as the best of King Mattu's hordes of conquerors.

Akhu now stood as tall as One Eye, not as broad in the shoulders but with arms as thick as his muscular legs, arms that slashed a broad sword more swiftly and deftly than any who had faced it. Akhu was a prime example of the perfect soldier, skilled beyond his years, faithful to his leader, and smart, a boy destined for greatness if he lived through the awful years of ferocious combat.

Though the Sea People never ventured far from the Mediterranean and all the riches it provided, they had begun meeting up with advancing

Roman units probing the defenses of the countries of Africa.

"I have no doubt that the Romans want Alexandria as it is the richest city on the Sea," Akhu said one evening as they sat by a cooking fire overlooking the vast Mediterranean below. "Why would they not want it more than the poor lands to the east?"

"The Greeks have been here for ages. They are strong," One Eye said. "We are their friends most of the time. They will keep the Romans away. They will not let anyone take the city that their Alexander founded long ago."

"As you say, the Greeks are strong but the Romans and their short swords and Legions in perfect formation have swept across the north. They will look for more to conquer. Believe me."

"My young friend, I grow old and tire of this fighting. Will these battered bones never see the peace we both long for?"

"I'm afraid that is not what the gods want. Osiris, the god of the underworld wishes otherwise."

Akhu sat back and saw his friend doze off, then his gaze swept out over the Mediterranean, first up along the coast to the east that held the lands they had invaded, sacked, looted, and then turned to the left, to the west where, far away, his boyhood home of Alexandria lay. He closed his eyes, listening to the gulls squawking above, and tried to remember.

His mother and father's faces were hard to recall but that of his sister, Sabra, was as clear as the day they had parted. Beautiful Sabra. A shudder ran through him as he thought of that awful moment when he watched men pick her up and drag her away, to what end he had only the most frightening images. In every town, every village, on every fighting expedition, he had watched young girls hauled away by his soldiers who did unmentionable things to them as spoils of war.

All he could hope for was that someone had taken pity on her and saved her from rape and death.

A messenger arrived, waited a moment for One Eye to wake and sit up then handed him a parchment. He gave it to Akhu who read it twice and folded it in half.

"The king has ordered us to join our ships. We sail for Cyprus and a city of gold."

Chapter Seven - Sabra's Conquest

Weeks passed. Sabra was allowed complete freedom of the compound, an array of houses, commercial buildings, stables, along with the main house, a settlement that resembled a small city.

Saul, the Jew from the Holy City, sat in an elevated chair in an assembly hall crowded with soldiers, a few merchants, and no women.

Outside, Sabra waited, her ear pressed to the wood door so she could hear what her master was up to now.

The voices were muffled but she was able to understand. The discussion was about a message from the Egyptian King, Nebrunef, a message asking for a truce.

"Why would the Egyptian King ask such a thing of us?" a voice said. "They hate us."

"Do they wish us to be lulled into the idea of peace and then be crushed if we came to their city?" another asked.

"I suspect it is the Romans that have him worried. The Greeks have become soft and are only interested in government and taxes not war," a voice said.

All it took was a conversation like this to remind her of her beloved Alexandria and family. As she listened to the discussion in the other room, her thoughts went to that other life she'd lived, the one of innocence and youth now gone.

Saul had won her over, slowly and skillfully. His intelligence and interest in things foreign had, at first, intrigued her and brought about many conversations. Soon, however, she felt his influence on her heart. He was good to her and never pressed his obvious intentions until one night the conversation turned to slavery.

"You do not treat me like the other slaves," she had said.

"I don't think of you as one but as an intelligent and beautiful woman."

"Am I really beautiful?"

"Like no other I have ever seen."

She had looked down at her arms that were no longer skinny but full and smooth, at her lap, the thin linen cloth stretched across thighs as perfect as the marble statue in the main hallway, the one she often looked at and compared to her bursting body.

"You have no idea how lovely you are, do you?" he said.

"I only hope I please you."

He leaned back on his pillows and smiled.

"You please me a great deal."

But, you can have any girl you want. Why do you say these things to me? It upsets me."

"I hope it upsets you in the right way," he said smiling again. "Of course, I can have any of the girls or women but I prefer to spend my time with you."

"Because I am smart and you like to argue with me or because you like to look at me like you are right now?"

For a moment he said nothing then got a serious expression on his face, his eyes boring into her as if searching her mind for answers.

"I want you in ways you could not imagine."

She rose, smoothing the thin linen dress on her thighs as she got up. For a moment, she stood in front of him, delighted at the way he looked at her, the way his black eyes roamed up and down, wondering what thoughts ran though his mind. Then she stepped forward and took his hands in hers.

"I want to learn these things you know. I want to learn them now."

Standing, he led her into his chambers.

That was a few weeks ago. Now, as she stood listening to the men inside the assembly hall discuss the Egyptian's king's offer, her mind kept going back to those days and nights with him.

Saul had been gentle and slow. In fact, now that she thought about it, he'd let her find her way, had let her touch and feel, find what pleased her and what frightened her. Soon, nothing frightened her and she found herself experimenting, looking for new ways to make him happy.

Saul, smitten beyond control, dismissed all his other girls and kept only Sabra. Occasionally he brought his wife to his bed though never together.

Before the fall season changed, he granted her freedom from her slavery and told her she could go to her home in Alexandria if she wished.

"I cannot leave you, my love," she said. "Our lives are entwined though we have this eternal problem of worshiping different gods."

Chapter Eight - The Assyrians

Another year passed. Akhu was wounded defending his friend, a fight between a dozen of the Sea People and almost a hundred Assyrians who caught them as they were about to board their boat. Twelve men fought until the bodies were piled up around their small circle. Blow after blow brought down one Assyrian after another but the toll was heavy. Soon. only four Sea People stood back to back. A sudden slash from behind caught Akhu on the arm. He spun around and drove his long sword into the attacker's throat but the soldier he'd been fighting stabbed him in the side before the man was chopped down by One Eye.

The two men looked at each other for a moment, both realizing this was the end of their long road of friendship, then both turned back toward the bloody fight.

A horn sounded followed by the sound of a dozen hoof beats. The Assyrians turned to face another group of Sea People galloping down the hillside, comrades who'd been late to reach the boats. Swiftly, the Assyrians were chopped down but not before Akhu fell at One Eye's feet.

Quickly, he was picked up and placed in the boat which shoved off for their ship at anchor.

Taken below, Akhu was treated for his wounds but soon dropped off into a deep sleep from a potion given him by the ship's medical man.

One Eye, bloody and dirty from the battle, sat by his side, holding his friend's limp hand and muttering pleas to the god of mercy.

Another attempt was to be made against the fortress of Cyprus but One Eye would be going into battle without his closest friend who lay in a deep coma. The Surgeon shook his head as if to say it was hopeless.

"Will it never end?" One Eye whispered to the inert body spread out on the bloody bench.

Chapter Nine - Departure for Jerusalem

"A surprise," Saul said coming into their room, waking her from an afternoon nap.

He sat on the edge of their bed, looking down at the magnificent body of Sabra laying back on her pillows, not caring if he saw her totally naked in broad daylight.

For a moment he hesitated then, seeing her smile and those beautiful searching eyes, went on with his surprise.

"We leave at day break for Judea, the Holy Land, where you will see the great marvels of God's creation."

She smiled and took his hand, placing it on her breast.

"I find no place more marvelous than this bed."

"But, you must see it. Jerusalem is the most sacred city in the world. People come from all over to be where the miracles occurred. A Rabbi must go"

"There are no miracles, only those events destined by the gods."

"We shall see," he said removing his tunic and approaching the bed.

Chapter Ten - Suffi

Akhu opened his eyes. A young, black woman held a cloth to his wound.

"Where am I?" he asked in a hoarse voice.

"You are on your ship. We arrive in Cyprus two days from now. But your master says you will not join them and I agree."

He looked at her again, a beautiful, young woman as black as the darkest night but whose eyes were as white as the whitest sand.

"Who are you to tell me what I cannot do?" he asked.

"I am Suffi, a slave like you and given the task of making you live again. I have been by your bedside for three days."

"Three days?" he shouted then coughed from the pain.

"You have been in a deep sleep. The potion is strong but, by the tone of your voice, it seems to have been successful."

He leaned back and let her bathe the wound in his side. Looking down, he saw the deep slash below his ribs, a jagged cut that had been sewn with thin, linen thread.

"Am I going to be all right?" he asked in a softer voice.

She smiled, bright white teeth, soft sympathetic eyes, and nodded yes.

"Suffi. Is that right? I am to call you Suffi?"

"Yes. That is my name but you may call me whatever you wish."

"I like it. Suffi it is."

She smiled again and leaned back. What he saw was a very black girl almost as tall as he was, thin but with a buttocks and breasts that were all but bursting out of a white, wraparound tunic. Her hands had long fingers, each one with tattoos up and down on top, symbols that looked like his native hieroglyphics. On her cheeks were raised welts in orderly rows as if burned into her young skin on purpose.

"You look at these," she said fingering the raised marks on her cheeks."They are done to all girls in my tribe when our first time comes. I hope they do not offend you?"

"No, they are quite pretty. I like them."

She smiled and softly moved the cloth along the caked blood on his side.

He lay back down and let her take the pain away, listening to her hum a soft melody.

"Ah ha," sounded the rough voice of One Eye as he burst into the small cabin. "You live to fight again."

"It will be some time before he can hold a sword," Suffi said looking up at the huge man as he barged into the cabin.

"And already having a wench in your bed?"

"No. No. Nothing like that," Akhu said.

"And why not?" One Eye replied, "If she is not to your liking you may send her to my cabin."

"I am with Master Akhu and sworn to make him well again," she said with her head down.

"Yes, One Eye. I need her. Do not interfere."

He howled with laughter.

"Just the medicine you need. But, I tarry too long. A storm is coming. You must tie yourself in as the seas will be rough and we don't want to open that wound again."

"I will see that it is done," Suffi said coming to him and wrapping a lanyard around and under his body, tying him to the bench so he wouldn't fall.

"Good." One Eye said and left the cabin.

Within the hour, the wind howled and the ship tossed on huge waves. Shouts came from above. Water poured down the hatch and the ship rolled and slammed into waves that made life below decks more miserable than for those out in the storm. The cabin heaved far to one side then seemed to hover as if thinking of continuing then slowly rolled back the other way. All the while the bow plunged into larger and larger waves, crashing down and sending sheets of spray over the men struggling on deck. More than one was swept overboard even though they were all seasoned sailors.

As darkness fell, Akhu looked at the wet floorboards below his bench and shook his head.

"We have to get up on deck," he said trying to sit up. "Look at all that water."

He pointed to the floorboards that were covered with sea water and getting deeper as he spoke.

"She's going to sink. We must get up on deck."

"But you cannot walk. Your wound? It will open."

"Would you rather we drown?" he said swinging his legs off the bench and attempting to stand.

She rushed over, put his arm around her shoulder, hers around his waist, and struggled with him toward the stairs that led above.

Step by step, she pushed and shoved, finally getting him up and out into the howling wind and rain. Holding him upright, she tried not to bump into his wound, and led him to the rail. Below, two boats filled with men, were already in the tossing sea, men paddling with their hands, frantically trying to get clear of the sinking ship.

"What do we do?" she asked in a surprisingly calm voice.

He looked up and down the deck then pointed to a bale of cotton strapped to the rail. Quickly, she drew a sharp dagger from within her tunic and slashed at the bindings freeing the bale that floated toward them on the slippery deck.

"Throw it overboard," he shouted.

She bent over, wrapped her long arms around the bale of cotton, and heaved it up and over the side.

"Jump. Find it and hang on. It will float."

"But I cannot leave you," she screamed over the wind.

"You must go now."

She stepped closer, looked calmly into his eyes, smiled, and struck him hard on the chin with her fist, toppling him over the side.

Immediately, she dove in after him, grabbed his arm and dragged him to the cotton bale where they both held on. Wave after wave beat at them, tore at their feeble grip but they held tightly with the determination of two who refused to die.

Two hours later, with lightning and thunder flashing all around them, she still gripped him tightly, her long arm around his shoulders, fingers dug into the wet cotton, and supporting his head above water.

Dawn came slowly, grey and ominous, but the storm was finally over. Suffi held a half conscious, Akhu, in her arms, the cotton bale all but underwater, now a soggy mass of fibers slowly peeling apart.

"Look," she shouted and nodded toward the sun.

Akhu barely heard her voice but opened his eyes to see land weave in and out of focus, a cliff of yellow sand that sloped down into the water.

"There is no place to land," she said. We must swim for it."

"No. Stay with the raft. I cannot swim."

Huddled together on the half submerged bale of cotton, they waited as the waves pushed them closer and closer to the sheer cliff.

"That rock," she said. "We can hold onto it."

She pushed his head back, wrapped her arm under his chin, and swam him away from the raft. Stroke by stroke, she dragged his body through the surf, most of the time her head under water but always with his high and free.

Coughing, spitting up salt water, she reached with her free hand and grasped the rock with her long, tattooed fingers. For another hour, she held them in the swirling sea until the sun rose high and poured its warmth onto them.

A face peered over the cliff, that of a young shepherd boy who took one look and disappeared. After what seemed like ages, other faces stared down at them. One man then another jumped into the sea and towed them around the cliff to a small cul-de-sac beach. Other hands carried them to a small encampment and the warmth of a fire. Women in strange clothing wrapped them in rough blankets and spooned hot liquid into their mouths.

Akhu woke, slowly opened his eyes, and stared at the naked, black body of Suffi, kneeling by his side. He started to speak but she smiled and touched his mouth with those exquisitely, long tattooed fingers.

"Do not speak. You are safe but have slept for two days. I have been with you."

He could hardly believe his eyes and wondered if he was dreaming. Beautiful beyond anyone he had ever seen, she kneeled next to him, leaning over, spooning a sweet liquid into his mouth, her smiling face, radiant, large, bare breasts hanging down and touching his chest as she fed him.

"Suffi, thank you," he whispered in a raspy voice. "I feel like I'm dreaming."

She smiled, her breast rubbing across him as she reached for a cup of cooked grain.

"Where are we?"

"After the ship went down, the roaming people rescued us from the sea. They call themselves Bedouin or gypsies. We have heard of them in my land but I have never seen them before. They wish to move on but I have pleaded with them to wait until you are well enough to travel."

He felt his head swim and the vision in front of him blurred and went dark.

Water ran down his cheek as he opened his eyes to look into the sweet, smiling face of Suffi.

"You are back. It is good," she said mopping his brow with a wet cloth. "You have slept another day."

Laying on his good side, he stared at the naked, black body of Suffi still kneeling by his bed pad then realized he too was completely naked. Her fingers squeezed a wet cloth making water run down his cheek, his neck, and onto his chest, her careful nursing avoiding the healing gash in his side as she cooled his fevered body.

"That feels wonderful," he whispered.

"It is unbearably hot plus your fever. But why do you stare?"

"You are amazingly beautiful. I never guessed what was under your tunic."

"Ah, the man is getting better," she laughed running the cloth up and down his legs, the cooling water evaporating almost as soon as it touched his hot skin.

"In my tribe," she said, "children do not wear clothes until they become adults. It is very hot in Thebes. Women never wear anything on top like you Egyptians. I feel more at home like this."

He leaned back letting her hands soothe his fevered skin and looked more closely at her sweat drenched, black body noticing that around her nipples were raised welts radiating out like petals of a flower.

"What are they?" he asked softly.

She looked down, touched one of them, and smiled.

"At the time of womanhood, all girls are branded here with a hot iron. It is a sign of great beauty. I wished to have more petals on my breasts than any other girl. Do you not like them?"

"It is unusual but very pretty."

The flap leading to the outside opened and an old woman came into the tent, stooped over, and touched his forehead.

"He is better," she said.

"Yes." Suffi replied looking up at the woman's wrinkled, dark face.

"I will tell the elders. We will leave tonight so as to travel when it is cooler."

"As you wish, madam."

The woman nodded and left the tent.

"Where are we headed," Akhu said trying to sit up with Suffi's help.

"They have told me we are headed to the city of Jerusalem, a four day ride from where we are on the coast."

"So it will be Jerusalem not Cyprus," Akhu said still unable to take his eyes of the glistening, perspiration drenched, blackness of Suffi.

Night came and their tent was taken down, packed with others in tight bundles and loaded onto waiting camel's backs. Suffi, dressed in a white, wraparound tunic and sandals, helped an identically dressed Akhu onto an old, female beast.

He groaned at the pain in his side but, with her help, sat astride the old camel and gripped the leather saddle. Like an agile cat, she swung up behind him, her hands around his waist and bare legs pressed against his thighs. Even though still far from recovered, he felt her body against his back and an unfamiliar feeling stir in his chest.

A whistle came from a man at the head of the column and the camels plodded off into the night.

It took hours for him to become comfortable with the swaying, lurching movement of the beast but eventually it became like second nature. He smiled feeling her breasts against his back, her hands clenched around his waist, and the soft, murmuring noises coming from her mouth as she slept, a deep sleep, possibly the first she'd had since their rescue.

He knew little about Suffi, only that she too was a slave but that was all in the past now. They had escaped the sinking ship and their master and could no longer be considered slaves of the Sea People. He remembered she had told him she was from a tribe deep in the desert in a place called Thebes, a primitive tribe from what it sounded like but she was educated and spoke well on many subjects. He'd have to ask her more about Thebes. But, there was something else that bothered him. She had been told by their master to take care of him after he was wounded. Now, he was well. Why was she still at his side, still waiting on him, and not trying to escape, get back to her people?

She stirred, squeezed him around the waist, and pressed her legs even more firmly against his.

"Are you awake?"

Her sleepy voice said, "I just had a wonderful dream."

He smiled as the camel plodded on through the sand.

"We were in my land, in my family house. You sat with my father and drank from the cup. He was happy."

"Is that a custom to drink with the head of the house."

She laughed.

"Only when a daughter marries."

"You dreamt we got married?"

"Yes. Is it so awful to marry a black princess?"
He turned his head.

"I should not have said that. I am sorry," she said.

"You are a princess?"
She was silent for a minute.

"Yes. I am Princess Suffi, of royal birth, daughter of King Odrum."

"My god, what are you doing as a slave and with me?"

"I was captured by them and made a slave just as you were. But, I see a great man in Akhu, a man who will return me to my people."

A sandstorm, a delay finding an oasis with water, all gave Akhu more time to recover. By the third day on the trail, he felt well enough to dismount and jog alongside their camel, with every step gaining strength. On the fourth day, with Jerusalem in the far distance, he ran next to the beast, his long sword held high, and screamed at the devils who kept him from being a whole, fighting man again.

But, Suffi knew better. She saw the old Akhu, the one she favored, and smiled.

Chapter Eleven - Parade of the Legions

The small ship arrived in the port of Ashdod on the Mediterranean coast of Judea, called by the devout, the Holy Land. Sabra stood at the rail, her arm in Saul's, and looked up at his smile, his eyes staring at the sacred place.

"Do all Rabbi's have to make this pilgrimage?" she asked in a tiny voice almost afraid of the look of reverence on his face.

"It is required. Who will listen to the word of one who has not been in the arms of God?"

"But it looks just like all the other lands along the coast."

"It was chosen by God as the place of the miracle."

"How I wish my faith was as strong as yours, my love."

The anchor plunged into the sea and the ship came to rest.

Two hours later they were on the backs of camels, part of a caravan heading into the desert toward the city called, Jerusalem.

A two day journey brought them through the gates and into the sacred city, a place of adobe houses, busy streets, and the presence of Roman soldiers.

"There are Roman's everywhere." she said nervously holding his arm, always uncomfortable in the presence of armed men

"It is like I told you. Jerusalem is an open city, a place of welcome to anyone who wishes to make the journey here. They are merely pilgrims like us. Look there. That is where Moses walked."

Saul, though a wealthy, educated Rabbi, was like a child, pointing out this site, then that, his excitement bubbling over as they walked through the crowded streets, his nervousness increasing with every step. She clung to his arm, indifferent to the stares of the soldiers and strange men of unknown skin color, all dressed head to toe in foreign clothing. Sabra, content in Saul's loving protection, had no appreciation of how her ravishing beauty affected those who looked at her. She walked beside him in a long, skin tight linen dress, the neckline plunging to her waist, exposing a great amount of her olive toned breasts, the look of an Egyptian woman of means, one of standing, and education.

They walked rapidly toward the goal of their journey, the Holy Temple, the site of ultimate worship for all Jews.

His pace quickened as they rounded a corner and gazed up at the temple. Wood scaffolding encased the side where it had been burned in one of the many attempts to reduce it to rubble by invaders.

Saul kneeled on the steps and said a long prayer among other Jews who mumbled long, complicated messages to someone called Yahweh.

She stood next to his kneeling body, looking out at his beloved city, so strange to her, so different from Alexandria. Nothing she'd ever seen was quite like this. All around her men with beards lay flat on the steps, their foreheads pressed against the stone, all mumbling prayers in different languages. Among them, her Saul was lost in total concentration. She looked down at him and smiled. If it were not for Saul, she would have long ago found a way home to Egypt where everything was not so foreign and she could worship her own gods, those that she knew in her heart were the real gods.

A group of Roman soldiers stood under an awning near the steps of the Holy Temple, four armed men wearing short kilts, leather breast plates, leg guards, swords in sheaths at their waists, and decorated metal helmets on their heads. Their leader smiled at her which she unconsciously returned then wished she hadn't done so when he pointed her out to his men who laughed.

Saul saw none of this as his eyes were closed in deep prayer. But she knew he would have been angry, his rules of behavior so unlike those of Egyptians, rules that said women must be quiet and submissive. She thought of the burden it must have been a for him to allow her so much freedom to dress as she did and to speak up when she wanted to. As she stood there and waited, she wondered if he actually loved her?

"I see you are not one of these Jews," the Roman said coming up the steps and standing very close to her, the garlic on his breath like a cloud around him.

"Please do not bother him," she said quietly. "He is a Rabbi and is praying."

"He will not miss you then. Come into the shade with me. It is not good for a woman so beautiful to stand in this sun. I have never met an

Egyptian woman before and am pleased to find it is true what they say."

Not wanting to make a fuss and bother Saul, she followed him down the steps and under the shade of the awning.

"Ahh, this is better," she said looking at him sweating in the awful heat. "Is it not too hot out there for wearing so much armor?"

"Would you have me take it off? I will gladly do so if you wish."

"No. No. I meant it is so much for such a hot place," she said wondering why she was talking so openly with this man. "Thank you. This shade is most welcome."

The soldier stood terribly close, the same way men did in Egypt, a custom she had not enjoyed in a long time. He was quite handsome, young, and extremely muscular, thick bare legs, and biceps bulging out around the metal clasps on his arms.

"Why are you, such a beautiful Egyptian woman, with an old Jew?"

"He is my benefactor, a good man, and my friend."

The other soldiers laughed from where they stood nearby.

"And you are visiting this dirty city with him?"

"Yes, we will see all the famous temples and return home fortified by his God."

"Not your god, correct?"

"No. I believe in the Egyptian deities."

"We Romans also worship many gods. These Jews will learn someday."

"I'm afraid that will not happen."

He looked at her, stared down into the plunging neckline, the up into her radiant face, and smiled.

"There will be a large parade of my Roman Legion this afternoon. You are invited to watch the procession from the shaded grandstand. It will give me great pleasure to have my company salute you as we pass."

"I love parades and will ask my friend."

He walked her back up the steps to where Saul still kneeled, his concentration so great, he had not noticed her visit with the Roman soldiers.

"But it will be wonderful," she said holding his arm as they left a small cafe. When will you ever get to see a Roman Legion like this? I want to experience more than just temples. There is much to learn here."

He smiled and nodded his head, "All right but only for a short while."

"Thank you, my beautiful Saul," she said wondering why he hadn't commented about the sheer linen dress she wore, a dress of almost transparent cloth in the formal Egyptian style, a gown that showed much of her bare body beneath.

They were allowed seating in a shaded grandstand along the side of a wide avenue. Crowds stood everywhere but only well dressed and affluent looking people were seated in the shade. Along the street, the people of Jerusalem were massed shoulder to shoulder straining to see over each other's heads.

Trumpets sounded and a wide phalanx of soldiers in full armor appeared at the far end of the street, each man carrying an enormous flag that whipped in the hot, desert wind. On they came, followed by tight formations of one hundred armed men each, group after group of one hundred parading soldiers. Row upon row passed the grandstand, every man in exact, precise marching step.

As the sixth group of one hundred Legionnaires passed the grandstand, a shout broke the sound of pounding feet and every soldier's head snapped toward Sabra. then returned to face front at another shout from their leader, the commander she recognized as the man she'd spoken to at the temple.

Sabra turned red as all eyes fell on her.

"What is this all about?" Saul asked in a confused voice.

"A Roman I met while you prayed at the Temple," she said her face still flushed in embarrassment or worry.

Saul turned away and watched a troop of chariots led by white horses thunder by.

"I will never understand the freedom you Egyptian women think is acceptable and normal," he said taking her hand and leading her away from the parade.

Chapter Twelve - Jerusalem

Akhu led Suffi along a dusty road as they entered through the gates of the old city of Jerusalem among throngs of visitors, merchants, and travelers.

"There are many Roman soldiers," Suffi said as the camel plodded along the dirt road.

"Yes. They have advanced this far. The fear is that the Romans have Egypt in their sights as their next conquest. The Greeks have always been more friends than conquers and worked closely with the Pharaoh but that is not the way of the Romans. They wish to conquer, gain submission, then put their puppet governments in charge. All of Egypt should be worried now that they have come so near."

They followed the crowds, not knowing the city and thinking the mobs of people must be headed somewhere important. Soon, the crowds thickened. Akhu hobbled the camel, took Suffi by the hand, and led her into the masses of people standing by the side of the street.

"What is happening?" he asked a Bedouin standing near him.

"A parade. The Roman Legion of the South is to march by. Such a sight you have never seen before."

Akhu turned to Suffi, "Just as I suspected. We should probably leave and not be part of this."

"No. When will we ever get a chance to see a real Roman Legion?"

"Never, I hope."

"Please, Akhu I want to see them."

"This heat is blistering. If we were to stay we should be up there in those grandstands with the cream of Judean society." he said shading his eyes from the bright sun light. "But, that is not for ex-slaves like us."

They looked up at the well dressed crowd under awnings flapping in the desert breeze.

Trumpets sounded and a phalanx of Roman soldiers appeared holding flags on tall staffs, flags that whipped in the wind as they marched.

After them came groups of one hundred soldiers all in lock step and full armor. After a number of the groups had passed, one section, at the bark of a command, snapped their heads in salute to someone in the stands. All eyes followed to see who was getting such a tribute.

A beautiful young woman stood beside a middle aged man in Jewish clothing.

Akhu thought he'd never seen such a sight as what met his eyes, a young woman, in the thinnest, almost transparent, linen sheath, a body like nothing he'd ever seen before, and shining, blue eyes that met his for an instant then looked away.

"I wonder who she is?" Suffi said.

"Some Jewish woman of means, I suppose."

Chapter Thirteen - The Centurion

Saul left after the evening meal for an all night fast at the temple with other devout Jews. Sabra wandered downstairs and spoke to the innkeeper.

"Are there bath's nearby?'

"Yes, there is one only a short distance away," he said pointing. "Just down the lane."

"Thank you," she said.

The day had been hot and dusty. With Saul gone, she thought nothing could be more pleasant than to go to the public baths and soak away the dust and filth of the city.

She pulled her wraparound tunic tight and left through the entrance of the inn. A sign for the baths was soon visible on a large adobe building, a plaque attached on an adobe wall with an arrow pointing to the pleasures within.

An attendant took her coin and handed her a thin, cotton cloth, really just a sheet of cotton that she was to wear instead of her tunic. She entered a cubicle, dropped her tunic to the floor, wrapped the filmy sheet around her body, and wandered into a room that smelled of the sea. Sparkling in the soft light was a tiled pool filled with shimmering, blue water. Steam rose from the surface clouding much but not before she saw another woman come out of the water at the far end and leave for an adjoining room.

"This is perfect," she said. "Everyone is at their dinner hour and I have it all to myself."

She dropped the sheet to the tiles and stepped into the pool, sighing as she lowered her naked body into warm, clear water. A good swimmer, Sabra stroked her way across and back then noticed a sign over where the woman had left.

"A steam room. Even more perfect."

Climbing out, she wrapped the sheet around her wet body, walked into a hallway, and found a door with steam seeping out of the cracks . It opened easily and she stepped into a thick cloud of burning, hot fog, so thick that she could see nothing. Groping with her hands she found a series of stone steps that led up and remembered that the steam baths back in Egypt had similar steps. The higher you climbed, the hotter it got.

She sat on the lowest step, removed the covering sheet, and leaned back, the sweat already seeping out of her pores. Each breath drew searing, hot air into her lungs. In less than a minute her skin was soaked with perspiration, all glistening and shining in the dim light.

"Wonderful," she said to the swirling steam around her.

"I couldn't agree more," a man's voice said who appeared like an apparition out of the mist.

Though accustomed to seeing Saul undressed, she was startled at the vision in front of her only an arm's length away.

As naked as she, the Centurion stood with his arms on his narrow hips, his strong legs apart, his immense, muscle rippled body covered in sweat.

"You surprised me," she said trying to regain her composure though her heart pounded in her breast.

"I didn't mean to. Please forgive me. I too wanted to purge my body of the dust and dirt of our parade. Did you enjoy it?" he said stepping even closer.

Her voice didn't sound natural to her but she got out a feeble, "Yes."

"Did you like the salute my men gave you?"

"It embarrassed me but, yes, I did enjoy it."

"Why are you acting like this moment is less enjoyable?"

"I'm not. I mean... I don't know."

He stood so close she could almost feel the heat coming off his sweating body. Confused at the feelings pounding inside her, she bit her lip and took a deep breath.

"My friend would not understand. He is a Jew and does not enjoy the freedom you seem to expect."

"Do you mean the freedom to do this?" he said placing his damp hand on her belly. Then, with his dark eyes staring directly into hers, his hand slowly ran up her wet skin, up and under her breast, cupping and lifting it, then smiling. "You are the most beautiful woman in all Judea, maybe even in Rome."

"Thank you," she said in a whisper, her heart pounding beneath his hand, his wet thigh touching hers.

Almost faint with desire, she moved into his arms and let him draw her close. Nothing clouded her thoughts, not Saul, not Akhu, nothing, as the steam swirled around them and he lay her down on the stone bench.

Sabra lay on her bed pad at the inn waiting for Saul's return. She was sore from head to toe, her body red and chafed from the intense heat of the steam room and the rough stone where they had made love.

How would she explain this to her man, a Jew who spoke of her loyalty often. Though Saul had a wife and a few slaves who used to come to his bed, he had stopped that and slept only with her. But, she wasn't his wife and he had no claim on her as she was now free. He just accepted the fact that she was his.

But, as she lay there, she realized that now, more than ever, her values had changed. She had been exposed to much more than even the most open minded Egyptian. She was no longer the young girl that had loved only Akhu. She had been a slave, a mistress of Saul's, and now the willing sexual partner of a Roman Centurion. But her conscience bothered her. What would Saul think? What would Akhu think?

The fact that she had sworn on her god, Isis, the goddess of fertility, that she would always be honest with Saul was almost worse than the feeling of wanting the Centurion again and again until she could barely breathe.

Dawn came. The fast would be over and Saul would return to the inn, tired and hungry. She got up pulled on one of his linen skirts and fed the fire so she could prepare him a morning meal. She tore a piece of bread and put it on the small table, poured a cup of water and snapped a large cluster of grapes from a twig hanging from a rafter.

The sun was well up when he came into the small room and sat at the table where she served him his water, bread and grapes.

"Did the fast go well?" she asked.

He turned to look at her and frowned.

"Why are you so red? You look like a cooked animal."

"The innkeeper told me of a nearby bath. I went and spent too long in the hot room. I almost died of the heat."

There, I've told him the truth, she thought.

"But you have scratches on your arms and a mark on your neck."

Her hand went to her neck, a bite mark she's missed when she put on her makeup this morning.

"I cannot lie to you, Saul. I was with the Centurion, the one ..."

"You gave yourself to a stranger?"

"Yes. Please forgive me. He was quite insistent."

He ate one grape after another and wiped his mouth with his arm.

"You were my slave. I freed you, gave you my bed, and you willingly came to sleep in it. Why would you defy me like this?"

She looked at the floor and all but whispered.

"I could not control myself."

Saul stared at her for a full minute, grabbed his piece of bread and left the room.

She sat on the floor, her head in her hands, and cried. Ten minutes later, she leaned back and wondered what Saul would do to her. He was not like other men. He wanted her to be faithful to him and only him. Other men had many women and their women enjoyed different men. Why didn't he understand?

Two hours went by. There was a soft knock on her door. She stood, pulled a skirt over her body, and opened the latch unprepared to face Saul.

Cassius, the Centurion, cradling Saul in his massive arms, entered the room and lay him down on the bed pad.

"He came to me at the camp. How he found me I have no idea?" Cassius said looking down at a limp Saul. "He struck me with a stick. I tried to reason with him but he kept pounding me with his staff. My guards heard the shouting, ran in, and drew their swords as his stick came down on my head. I am afraid he is dead. I am sorry. I tried to reason with him."

Sabra dropped to the floor, not caring that her skirt fell away, and held Saul's head in her hands.

"Oh, Saul. I am so sorry. I have failed you. Look what it has done?."

"You must come with me. It cannot be found that a visiting Centurion has killed a Rabbi in Jerusalem. Come."

She stood, realizing the danger they were in, pulled on a thin, linen dress, gathered her small bag that sat at the foot of the bed, looked sadly at Saul, and followed Cassius out the door.

Sabra rode in a carriage drawn by two horses. Around her were ten other women sitting on benches, prostitutes, slaves, a couple of children, all following their man who was a member of the marching squads of armed, battle hardened, Roman Legionnaires.

Cassius had told her she must stay with the women, and keep out of sight. His men, though loyal, were soldiers and used to taking whatever they wanted, whenever they felt like it.

It had been fortunate that Cassius, on returning to his unit with Sabra, had been instructed to take forty of his one hundred and march west from Jerusalem to probe the defenses of the Egyptians. Cassius rightly figured his advance probe was in preparation for a massive invasion by the Roman Legions to take Alexandria and all of Egypt.

She lay back amid the stares of the prostitutes and slave women, trying to absorb all that had happened. Her body was sore and bruised. She felt sorry for dear Saul, a man she had loved for his kindness to her but not for the feelings that raced through her body now. A smile crossed her face as she thought of the wild time she and Cassius had spent together.

He had taken her hand and all but dragged her away from the dead body of Saul, led her through the dark streets of Jerusalem, and into the first inn he encountered. A coin was placed in the inn keepers hand before he led her up some steps into a small room with a single bed.

Out of breath at the suddenness of his decisions, she had stood by a tiny window looking out at the quiet street when a hand ran around her waist and slipped inside the tunic's opening to touch bare flesh.

It was all so fresh in her memory, how a shiver ran through her and her breath came in short gasps. Never had anyone made her feel like this, not Saul, not anyone. For a brief second, she thought of Akhu, who as a child had given her the chills when they touched, but this was beyond anything mortal. Her face flushed, her arms broke out in little bumps like a chill might cause. Her heart pounded so loud, it could be heard.

"There is no woman this side of heaven like you," he had whispered in her ear. "I have never touched such flesh, such perfection."

Five hours later, she lay back, covered in sweat, her body bruised and torn but with a smile and enjoying a feeling she'd never had before.

"What have you done to me?" she had whispered.

"I have made love to the most beautiful woman on earth."

"You have only made a slave of me, a willing slave, a woman who will spend every day and every night making you happy. By the gods, you are not human. I have never..."

"Shh. lie back. I have more to show you," he'd said.

The caravan of marching men and the wagons carrying the women, made camp in a ravine between two high, sandstone cliffs. No fires were lit as Cassius's troops were deep in Egyptian territory. Jerusalem lay far behind across endless sand. A week of marching at double pace had brought them to the edge of the Red Sea. It was Cassius's plan to penetrate deep into Egypt near Cairo. If the Pharaoh had defenses they would be near the tombs, the pyramids of the dead, the sacred land of the Egyptians.

Sabra waited naked under a sheet in their small tent at the edge of the encampment. She had bathed her body and patted oils onto her skin, aromatic oils that he loved to massage into her warm body.

As always, her heart pounded at the thought of what he would do to her. She could almost see the image of him standing in the open flap, broad shoulders, massive chest and arms, legs of iron, standing in the fading light, removing his armor, every bit of him exposed except for the object of her passion hidden under a cotton, loin cloth.

She lay back, breathing rapidly, quietly listening for his footsteps.

Instead, she heard a fierce yell then the blast of a horn. Men shouted and the noise of swords clanging against each other filled the night air. Screams came from outside her tent, the screams of dying men then the thundering sound of horse's hooves.

Terrified, she jumped up and parted the tent flap. All around, men were fighting for their lives as hordes of Egyptian soldiers raced into the campsite on horseback, swords slashing, cutting down everything in their path.

In the center of the camp, Cassius stood, his body bloody, five Roman soldiers battling beside him as more than twenty Egyptians hacked at them from horseback. Ten Egyptians fell for every Roman, but soon Cassius stood alone, as men on horses circled around, swords pointing at his chest, slowly drawing closer as he stabbed out, hitting one or two but finally dropping to his knees. Exhausted, he held his sword high with arms covered in blood, his face grim but determined.

The horses stopped their circling and the Egyptian leader moved his mount forward. Cassius tried to raise his sword but couldn't. He stared up at the Egyptian then looked toward the tent where Sabra hid, smiled, and lowered his head. The Egyptian's sword came down and the huge body of Cassius fell forward into the sand, his head rolling toward the horse's hoof.

Sabra screamed and reached for her dagger under the bed pad. In only a few moments, the flap drew aside and two soldiers entered. Still naked from when she had waited for Cassius, she stood and charged at them but her wrists were grabbed and she was dragged out into the glare of burning tents and dying men.

The leader, still on his horse, looked down at her nakedness and smiled.

"At least we will get something from this night," he said. "Take her but do not touch her. She will bring us a fortune if we bring her to him as she stands."

"Take your hands off me," Sabra shouted. "I am an Egyptian like you."

"Ha. So they all say. Bring her and be careful the way you handle this prize or I will make your punishment pure agony," he said to his men. "She is going to make us rich. I know beauty when I see it."

Chapter Fourteen - Thebes

"I have four of our gold coins left," Suffi said as they sat sipping tea in a small Jerusalem cafe along the route the parading Roman Legion had long since passed by.

"But, the gypsies took all my coins," Akhu said. "How do you have...."

"I hid them in a place no man would look."

She placed the coins on the small table next to their cups of beer and smiled.

"We have no place to go," Suffi said. "You and I are nothing but strangers here in Jerusalem. Let us use these coins and go to my home."

"You would take an Egyptian to Thebes? They hate us there."

"I am a princess, do you not remember? What I say will be listened to."

"It is far."

"I would like to show you the place of my birth."

"The camel. We still have the camel?" he said.

"No. We should go by boat on the Nile. It is a long voyage to the first cataract then a longer one to the second before we get to Thebes."

"Yes, Princess, as you command."

She smiled and gave him her hand. They left the cafe to sell the camel at the market, an old worn out beast but one that knew the desert better than the young ones.

By nightfall they had booked passage on a lateen rigged, Nile boat carrying sheep up the Nile to the First Cataract. Suffi and Akhu sat on a bale of cotton that was strapped to the deck, watching the frightened sheep who were tied tightly to the single mast.

"This is hardly the way a princess should travel," Akhu said looking around at the grim conditions of the animal boat.

The smell of the sheep and the sweat coming from the bare cheasted crew were stronger than the soft wind that blew across the open deck. The captain gave them a dirty blanket which Akhu wrapped around their bodies as darkness fell and the river air got suddenly colder.

She handed him a piece of bread which he nibbled quietly as they watched the stars come out one by one.

"What will your family think when they find I am Egyptian, a white man?" Akhu asked.

"They are good people and will understand I have found a man outside our customs."

She put her hand on his bare thigh and squeezed.

"I wish the blanket was larger, then we could..."

Akhu smiled at this woman who was more beautiful than even his childhood love, his sister, Sabra. His mind wandered as he once again wondered what had happened to her after they were separated so long ago? Was she even still alive?

Almost as if she was reading his mind, she said, "You will find our customs quite like yours even though our lands are far apart. We marry but it is not necessary. Our lives are very open and free. But those who do marry never do so with close relatives like you have said Egyptian royalty often does. It is not done because when brother and sister marry, the child is often not right."

He nodded that he agreed. It had often been so in Egypt.

"But, you have said a man can have many wives in Thebes?" he said changing the subject away from how loving Sabra had often bothered his thoughts.

"Yes, many wives, some who can afford it have three or four. Some of our women even have more than one husband."

"We do not in Egypt. Once a man marries he stays with that one woman."

"We also have men with men. It is very common. My brother lays with my uncle."

He listened but saw that this, like other things was something different between their two worlds.

She went on, "All families have slaves, men who work in the fields and women who serve their master but they are treated well."

"When you are back as a princess, will you decide that I am but one of the many men you want, just one of many?"

"That is up to the gods, my love. It is up to the gods to decide who will be with who. How else have we come to be together."

"You are very wise, Suffi."

She snuggled close and placed his hand on her breast.

At the first cataract, they rode donkeys around the roaring rapids and boarded another smaller but cleaner boat. The crew of four men watched with leers and made comments in a foreign language as Akhu helped Suffi on board. He would have to be very careful and be on watch all the time.

Though he arrived in Thebes tired from his vigil, he smiled at her excitement. It had been four years since she'd been taken as a slave. Her family had no idea if she was alive or dead.

They stepped off the boat into a crowd of black faces, both men and women stripped to the waist, all sweat covered in the blistering Upper Nile heat.

Women passed holding bundles on their heads, breasts of all sizes bouncing as they walked. Men, wearing short skirts or loin clothes labored at the dock, their black bodies glistening in the sun.

"I am home, my Akhu. Come. We must find Mishi."

"Who is that?"

"My mother. She will be at the house."

She took his hand and led him down a long dirt path into the town, past a temple for some strange god, a goat's head above the entrance, then along narrow lanes, and up a hill toward a large, earthen building.

She reached through a wood gate and released a latch. Akhu followed her into a large courtyard filled with aromatic flowers and budding trees.

A scream came from a balcony landing above and thudding feet ran down wood steps to the courtyard.

"My daughter. My daughter. May Atem be blessed. The gods have answered my prayers."

A woman, no older than forty, as beautiful and full bodied as Suffi, and just as black, ran toward her and swept her off her feet.

"Mother, it is truly me."

"I knew this day would come," she cried and hugged her daughter.

Akhu stood back and watched as the two beautiful women hugged for many minutes. By the time Suffi's mother stepped aside, a small group of young children had gathered around them. Suffi spoke to each child and gave them a hug. Then she turned and took Akhu's hand.

"This is Akhu. You will all welcome him. He has saved my life many times when we were slaves together."

The mother looked at Akhu then back at Suffi who wore a wide grin, looked back at Akhu, her gaze sizing him up from bare head down across his skirted waist to sandaled feet. He instantly felt the distaste in the woman's mind that her daughter had brought home a white man.

But, though she tried to hide her emotions, Suffi's mother nodded her welcome. One of the youngest children came to the mother, reaching with his hands for her bare breast. She sat on a bench and gave the child her nipple to drink.

"You are welcome in our home," she said moving the child to her other breast.

"This is my mother, Mishi," Suffi said. "I have six brothers and sisters now, two more than when I left."

She turned to Mishi and asked, "Is my father..."

"He is off at war. The new ones are in the fields."

"You now have more than one husband?"

"Yes, daughter. It is very expensive to care for a large family when the oldest daughter disappears."

Suffi smiled that she understood.

Mishi looked at Akhu, her stare just below his waist.

"Is he aware of ..."

"No, mother. He will be our guest and nothing else."

The woman smiled and looked again at the strapping, white man her daughter had brought home.

A boy, around ten years old, ran into the compound shouting her name. On a leash, a sleek looking Jaguar ran by his side.

Suffi screamed and ran to the animal, hugging and squeezing it as it licked her face with a pink tongue.

"He remembers me. How wonderful. You have taken good care of him, Yaki. I am proud of you. And look how you have grown."

The boy bowed his head and smiled.

"We must prepare the evening meal before the men return," Mishi said still sizing Akhu up with eyes as big and dark as Suffi's.

Akhu sat at an outdoor table watching as mother and daughter prepared the meal as if four years had not passed. He looked from one to the other. Mishi was as beautiful in face and body as

Suffi even though she had delivered six live children. Amazing, he thought. What an amazing looking woman.

Mishi was aware of his not so subtle glances and smiled. It wasn't often a handsome white man came to her house.

The men sat at the table and ate bread and drank beer. Not much was said as the new husbands didn't know Suffi and had only heard of her disappearance years ago. Suffi told endless stories of their adventures and how Akhu came from a learned family in Alexandria. The men, simple workers of the fields, nodded but didn't understand much of what was said.

Mishi, however, understood everything. Her mind was going a mile a minute at the prospect of a rich and powerful man in their family. She sat back, saying little, but drinking cup after cup of beer.

"We are but simple people here in Thebes but have been blessed by the gods with fertile land and fertile women. How many of your learned women in Egypt can boast of six children and look like me?"

"You are a very fine looking woman, Mishi," Akhu said.

"Mother, you promised."

"I promised nothing," she said looking from one husband to the next then smiling at Akhu.

"Come, I must show you something," Suffi said standing and taking his hand. "Do not listen to her."

Akhu nodded his head in thanks for the meal and followed Suffi into the back room of the house. In the cool, half darkness, she pulled her bed pad away from the wall and pried open a board under it with the side of her dagger. Inside, was a bundle the size of a child which she took out carefully and laid on the bed pad.

"This is my present to you for all the joy you have given me," she said unfolding the cloth wrap.

One by one, she handed Akhu scrolls tied with gold twine.

"What are these. They are beautiful and look very old."

"These are the scrolls of Thebes and ancient Nubia. My father gave them to me for safe keeping.

But, they will only rot in time buried beneath my bed. I want you to take them to your famous library in Alexandria."

"Suffi, these are priceless. Scholars have searched all over the Upper Nile for them. Do you realize what you have here?"

"They are yours now, a symbol of my love for you and for the knowledge they may carry."

He took her in his arms and whispered thank you over and over in her ear.

"You tickle my ear. Please take me to my bed. I have never had a man in this house."

He smiled and removed his loin cloth bringing a gasp from Suffi.

Days later, Akhu was in the field working with the two husbands. Suffi and Mishi brought bread and beer and called them to sit under a tree and share the meal.

Akhu, wearing a loin cloth like the other men, sat between Suffi and Mishi. Soaked in sweat, he downed a large cup of beer as fast as his thirsty throat could swallow.

"For a scholar and an Egyptian, you work the field well," Mishi said not taking her eyes away from his sweating body.

"Thank you. It feels good to work and sweat after so long riding on camels and being in strange cities."

"Are you familiar with the customs of Thebes?"

"You have many customs. Which one do you refer to?"

"The one of the head of the household?"

"Mother, I forbid you to do this."

She smiled at her daughter and went on, "Our ways may seem strange to you but it is a very satisfactory arrangement. I have told you of my husband who is off fighting a war somewhere and that I have two other husbands here who serve me very nicely. But, I am still a young woman, am I not?"

"You are very lovely, yes."

""You will come to my bed tonight and I will show how an experienced woman takes care of a man."

Akhu looked at Suffi who had her head down and was staring at her sandaled feet.

"But..."

"There is to be no question. Suffi will not interfere. It is my right and my duty to my gods to satisfy my hunger. It is the way it is written."

Little more was said as they finished the meal in silence. Akhu went back to the fields with the husbands as Suffi followed her mother back to the house.

They lay in bed together, Suffi in his arms, a sad expression on her face.

"Would you leave with me tonight?"she said. "I don't want to share you with my mother."

"Tonight?"

"Yes, now. We can run to the boats and take one down the river, go all the way to your Alexandria. I want to see your wonderful city."

Akhu, equally troubled by the strange custom of sharing, nodded.

They got up and dressed in wraparound tunics. She handed him a newly tied, cloth bundle holding the scrolls and picked up their small bag of worldly goods.

"Follow me quietly," she said tiptoeing out of the room and through the door into the night.

Chapter Fifteen - Alexandria

Sabra's heart quickened as the troop of Egyptian soldiers entered the gates of Alexandria. Bathed, scented, and dressed in a nearly transparent, linen gown, she rode in a cart behind two horses. Behind her and in front of her trotted twenty Egyptian soldiers led by the man who had taken Cassius's life. In a sack swinging by his horses side, was her lover's head.

It was hard to tell which emotion bubbled up more, her fear of the man with Cassius's head or the excitement of finally being home once again.

After four years of absence, Alexandria had changed as much as Sabra. The streets were more crowded, the faces strange and often foreign, the smells somehow different.

As they wound their way toward the palace, they passed the Mouseion, the Alexandria Library, where she and Akhu had grown up. Memories flooded her mind as so many familiar sights greeted her eyes. She wondered once again if he was alive somewhere, someplace? But she knew the answer was impossible to know or find out. She had changed so much she doubted he would recognize her or even like what he saw. The years had made her a beautiful woman but had taken much. No longer was she a pure and innocent little girl but one who had seen and done too much.

Guards questioned the lead horsemen after the procession came to a halt at the palace wall. Soon, they were cleared through the gates to the Kings palace grounds and led by a messenger to a small but richly decorated building.

A eunuch came out and handed the leader a sack of gold. The soldier, after counting the contents, handed him the sack containing the Roman's head, smiled and pointed toward Sabra. The eunuch nodded his approval, helped her out of the cart, and led her inside.

Twenty or thirty, well dressed and pretty girls were lined up on either side of a long, thin room. At the far end, and sitting in a golden chair, was King

Nebrunef. By his side stood a middle aged woman who wore the crown of the queen.

The eunuch nodded that she was to follow him. Confused and numbed by all that had happened, she did as asked and stood in line, ten women away from the king. As woman after woman was led forward to be interviewed by the queen, she looked around at the others waiting their turn and searching for some kind of explanation.

"What is happening?" she whispered to the girl beside her.

The girl, short and very pretty, looked at Sabra's simple gown with a frown and said, "He is choosing new ones for the court. Why do you not know this?"

A eunuch standing nearby gave them a forbidding look and Sabra went back to watching the interviews and trying to hear what was said.

Two of the first twenty had been selected and stood by the queen. The girl she'd spoken to was turned down. Sabra was next and stepped forward, her breasts bouncing and free in the opening of her long, linen dress, her naked body flowing like liquid underneath the filmy fabric.

She stopped when told to in front of the queen.

"What is your name and where are you from?" the queen asked as king Nebrunef stared at her exquisite body and rubbed his fingers around the oval at the top of the Ankh, a gold symbol of fertility.

"I am called Sabra and came from Alexandria, the House of Hepu. I have been gone for a long while and came back to find my family but have been brought here against my will."

"You are quite impertinent. I did not ask for more than your name and where you were from," the queen said.

"I have been a slave but am not used to this kind of treatment."

"A slave? Were you abused in any way that harmed your lovely body?"

"No, I would not allow that to happen."

The queen looked at the king and smiled. He nodded his head and Sabra was told to stand by the other two girls.

Chapter Sixteen - Akhu Returns

The trip down the Nile went without incident and Akhu and Suffi entered the magical city of Alexandria through the gates of Heaven.

"They won't recognize you, Akhu," Suffi said walking at his side.

"My father is old but will know me. I feel it in my bones."

"You left as a boy and are returning as a man, a good man with a black woman at his side. What will he think?"

"I don't know, Suffi. I don't know but we are close. I recognize that street. There, see those steps? They lead up to a courtyard surrounded by a dozen buildings housing all of the world's knowledge."

"And more now," Suffi said touching the bundle under his arm.

"Father will be pleased."

They climbed the steps and walked across the courtyard toward the main building that housed his family and the most valuable treasures.

"Much is different," he said looking around. "I hope all is well."

At the doorway, he announced himself to a servant whose eyes went wide when he said his name.

"Is that really you, master Akhu. Do you not remember me?"

Akhu looked more closely.

"You were Sabra's teacher. Old Tetri. Yes. I remember."

"Come, Master Akhu. He will be thrilled to see you."

The slave all but ran down the hallway to a doorway that Akhu knew well, a large room filled with tables where scholars read the scrolls.

The slave smiled and opened the door. A familiar musty smell of old documents filled the air as they stepped into the silent room. A few heads looked up then back at their reading. All was silent until a shout from the far side of the room.

"By Isis, is that you, my son?"

An old man, a loose toga almost tripping him, stumbled forward from a desk covered with open scrolls, a wide smile on his ancient face.

"It is I, father. I have come home."

The old man burst into tears and hugged his son to his narrow chest, his eyes closed in prayer.

Suffi stood by his side, a wide smile on her face as she watched the reunion of father and son.

"We must sit and talk," the old man said taking Akhu's hand and leading him out of the room.

"This is my friend, Suffi," Akhu said as his father shuffled down the hall, not responding.

He led them into a small room with two couches and a table between.

"Sit. Sit. You must tell me everything."

"First, is Sabra alive? Do you know anything about her?"

His father lowered his head and spoke in a small voice, "Yes, she is alive and well. It would have not been my decision but she is in the king's court, has risen to be second concubine under the queen. But. I have not seen her since she returned from the wilderness."

Akhu nodded his head, absorbing what his father had said, then turned and smiled at Suffi. At least his sister was alive but it saddened him to think of her as a concubine of the pharaoh?.

They talked for a half hour before Akhu lay the bundle on the table between them.

"This is a gift of the people of Thebes, Princess Suffi's people."

"I am so sorry but I have been carried away by my son's return," the old man said. "Welcome. A friend of my son is a friend of mine."

She bowed her head and smiled.

"She is as pretty as the goddess Seshat," the old man whispered.

"Seshat is the goddess of libraries and literature," Akhu said taking her hand, "a wonderful compliment if I ever heard one,".

"And what is this gift from Thebes?" the old man asked.

"The ancient scrolls of Thebes and Nubia," Suffi said in a low, reverent voice. "I have decided they must be in a safe place and what better than Alexandria's Mouseion library."

The old man's eyes watered again as he took her hand and pressed it to his lips.

"It is a priceless addition and will be given a place of great honor. I myself will study them."

She smiled and looked at Akhu who was more pleased than she had ever seen him.

"We feast tonight," his father said.

They sat in the courtyard on a bench, a cool breeze off the Nile comforting them after a huge banquet meal.

"Tell me about your sister?" Suffi asked. "Why is she a concubine of the King?"

"Our Pharaoh is the ultimate ruler. He is a living god and must have whatever pleases him. He has had many wives who have given him children. But, he also has slaves and some free women who are his concubines, his to do with as he wishes."

"Is there no way...."

"None. His rule is law."

"I get the feeling from all you have said about Sabra that you were extremely close as children?"

Akhu smiled remembering how terribly devoted they were as children and as young adults, and how just the thought of her made his heart beat faster. He also remembered how something had kept them apart when desire got too strong like the time when she kissed him on the lips.

"Yes, we were closer than most married people."

Suffi looked into his eyes and saw what was there.

"You still love her as a woman not just as a sister, am I right?"

"I haven't seen her in four years and she is now in the bed of the king," he said looking at her, "And I have you. What more could a man want?"

"Will you take me to the room of your youth as I took you to mine?"

Surprised, he looked at her, stood, took her hand, and led her inside toward the family quarters.

Days became weeks, pleasant days and nights where Suffi and Akhu spent most of their time together.

"I am pleased at what I see in you, my son," his father said late one afternoon in the reading room. "Tonight, at the temple of Sashat, the goddess of Literature, you will be made the assistant librarian of the Mouseion."

"Father, you honor me beyond my worth."

"Not so. You have proven a good scholar but, more importantly, a man of honor, one who will defend the sacredness of this place with your life if necessary. Am I correct?"

"I will, father. I will do as you have done."

Suffi, sitting at a table nearby and reading one of the Thebes scrolls, smiled. She was happy for her Akhu. They had moved past the eternal waiting she had endured to win his love and, as she felt her belly, realized she would soon give him a son. If it were not for the rumors that swirled around the city about advancing Romans, she would have been content for the first time in her life.

She hesitated, not wanting anything to change his mood, then decided to tell him of her fears while they lay in his bed.

"What will happen if they come?" she asked.

"The Egyptian armies are strong. They will defeat the Romans. Alexandria is a well fortified city, almost impregnable."

"Almost is not good enough when there are Romans."

"Do not worry. It is not good for the child. You should rest and think of good things not of foreign soldiers."

She smiled and lay his hand on her belly.

"Do you feel your son? He is strong. I can tell."

Akhu was summoned to the palace and brought into the King's chambers. The great man sat on a throne, four young women serving him, three others sitting on pillows at his feet.

Akhu bowed his head and stood ten arm's lengths away as was prescribed.

"As our new Librarian, you will search the scrolls for the most magnificent temple Egypt has ever built, then you will find experienced men to design my tomb so it is bigger and more grand than anything built before."

Akhu leaned forward, listening, trying to understand the full implications of his king's command.

"May I speak?"

"Yes, go ahead," the king said.

"I am but a poor librarian and know little of the great tombs."

"You have all of the world's knowledge in those buildings of yours. What use are they if you cannot find out what your King needs?"

Akhu nodded his head but heard a small gasp from one of the women sitting at the king's feet. He looked more closely. It was the beautiful girl he'd seen only for a moment at the Roman parade in Jerusalem some six months ago, a face and body he would never forget.

One of the kings attendants fanned the king with a huge leaf, scattering a fly that had buzzed by his face and annoyed the pharaoh.

"Are you able to do this thing for your King?"

"I will do as you ask," Akhu said looking only at the beautiful girl, risking all to see her better.

He backed away but not before the young woman had lowered her head and not concealed a smile. His face was contorted in confusion at the feelings racing through his body.

Chapter Seventeen - Sabra and Akhu

Sabra lay among the floating bubbles of her bath, a young slave girl washing her with a sponge.

"Is something wrong, Mistress?" the girl asked.

"It is as if I have seen a ghost, Juji, a reincarnation of a child I once knew."

"Who is this ghost?"

"A boy. No, a man now, a beautiful man who once owned my heart."

Juji leaned over the tub and whispered, "Does he still?"

Sabra splashed soapy water at the slave girl and laughed.

"Our king owns my heart as he should own all hearts," Sabra said standing and taking a towel from Juji. .

"He has asked for you to wear the green dress tonight," the slave said. "It is his favorite."

"Rub me with the oil from Nubia. I wish him to be in a good mood tonight."

"Yes, mistress," Juji said as she poured oil into her cupped hands and smoothed it on Sabra's body.

Sabra smiled at her, as loyal a slave as any friend could be. But an observer would have been shocked to see them. Juji could have been Sabra's twin they looked so much alike. Months ago, Sabra had looked all over the kingdom for someone who looked like her, a double to fill in for her when chance or opportunity presented a challenge. They had once even fooled the king who surprised them by coming to her rooms unannounced while Juji tried on some of Sabra's clothes.

He had burst into the room as Sabra, on her knees and wearing only a loin cloth, was adjusting the pleats of a long gown on the hips of Juji. She was laughing and making fun of the way the slave girl stood nervously, when their king stepped into the room.

"You look ravishing in that gown, my dear," he had said sitting in a chair and watching.

Sabra had smiled up at Juji and nodded her head indicating she should go along with the ruse.

Juji looked up and said in a soft voice, imitating her mistresses, "Please wait in my chambers. I will wash this kohl off and be in your arms in a moment."

The king had stood with a smile and gone into Sabra's bed chamber to wait for his consort.

"Does the tomb go well?" Sabra asked as she handed her king a cup of wine.

"I have five thousand workers there night and day yet the librarian says it will take a year to finish."

"But, there is no rush. The gods have protected you and will do so forever."

"You are sweet to say so but I age and will die like all the other pharaohs before me. Yet, my voyage to the after-life must be perfect."

"Tell me of this voyage? I am but a simple woman who does not know."

He took a sip of his wine and set it down.

"Come to me and I will explain."

She got up from the pillow and scooted up, facing him between his outstretched legs, a position that allowed him to fondle her breasts while he talked.

"All pharaohs are gods and must be cared for in the after-life as they are while living. The plans for the tomb are good. The place of our entombment will be filled with tables of food, our servants there to feed us. We will wear precious jewels and golden tunics as we celebrate life ever after. The priests say I have very little time left yet the work stumbles on. It must be finished when the time comes for me to meet Isis and sit by her side."

"What would you have me do, my king?"

"Can you make them move faster? Can you use your influence as second consort to make your King happy?"

"I will do as you ask. But now, please lie back and let me bring you peace."

Sabra spent the following day trying to figure out how she could help her anxious king? It would do well for her to make things go better as she was as much his favorite now as his wife. The politics of the court would change if she could help in this task.

She sat at her table applying kohl to her eyes and henna to her lips. Juji stood behind her holding the sheerest of the many sheer dresses she owned, one that left nothing to a viewers imagination.

"Is he here yet?"

"Yes, mistress. The librarian waits in the next room."

Slowly, Juji lowered the dress over her head, being careful not to smear the makeup or her hair.

Sabra stepped back and looked into the polished brass mirror and smoothed it on her perfect hips.

"I may as well meet him naked," she said pulling the gown away from where it stuck to her body.

The girl giggled having long ago suspected the librarian was the boy of her youth that she spoke of so often, a boy who was now a man, the one appointed by the king to design and build the pharaoh's tomb.

Sabra went to the door and felt her heart flutter in anticipation and remembering. She stepped into the room and looked at the shadow of a man silhouetted by the sun and staring out the window.

"It is you is it not?" she said in a faint voice.

He turned and gazed at her, his eyes filling with the vision in front of him.

"Yes, Sabra. It is me. I have thought of this moment every day since we parted five years ago."

"As have I. Oh, Akhu. if it only had been different. If only..."

"But that is not the god's plan. Our lives have gone in very different directions. You are the king's concubine and I am but a simple librarian."

She lowered her head and nodded, seeing the way his eyes devoured her body.

"I am not the sister you once loved, Akhu. I have seen and done much that would disgust you. I have been a slave and a mistress of a Jew. I loved a Roman soldier with most of my heart. I am now the second consort of your pharaoh. But, my breast still pounds when I look at you."

Akhu bit his lip and wanted to step forward and take her in his arms.

"I have done more and worse," he said," killed, and raped and done great harm to others. But, I have met a good woman, a woman from Thebes who shares my bed and carries my child."

"She is the black woman I saw at your side in Jerusalem?"

"She is the one," he said.. "By Isis, I knew it was you. No woman could have had the effect on me that you did that day. I looked up and saw the girl I've loved all my life, my half sister, as beautiful as always. You took my breath away. But, I thought it was a mirage, a dream, the gods playing with my mind in the heat of the sun."

"Yet, you stand here in front of me and will not step forward as you desire?"

Akhu reddened. Sweat formed on his brow as he looked at the near nakedness of Sabra and her magnificent body that stood only an arm's length away, a vision that had helped him through sickness, fended off death when he was stabbed, and carried him through a thousand lonely nights in the desert.

"Desire is something you and I have conquered before," he said. "Can we not handle it now? But, you tempt me as always. All I have to do is look at you and my knees tremble."

"Have you married this black woman?"

"No, but we have been faithful to each other."

"To this day, my Akhu. I have been part of the pharaoh's court and a member of the royal family. Are you aware of what that means?"

"That in the case of a royal, the coupling of close siblings is permitted?"

"Yes, not only permitted but necessary."

His mind reeled at what she said, He knew the royal family acted in their own way, oblivious to the common man and the custom of the sanctity of marriage. But he was also familiar with the wonderful fact that unmarried women practiced sex without commitment, practiced until they were accomplished lovers and worthy of marriage. All this flooded his mind as they stared into each other's eyes.

"Is this not dangerous to you as the king's consort? I feel he would not like this conversation."

Her face was flushed and she bit at her lip, her hand shaking with excitement.

"I take that chance," she said plunging over a cliff of desire.

"I must admit I have never seen anyone quite as beautiful as you," he said in a voice that cracked with emotion.

"And you the most handsome and desirable man in all of Egypt."

The two of them stood so close that he smelled the oils that glistened on her body, felt the heat coming from her skin, and her fragrant breath each time she spoke.

"Sabra, I must not."

"Yes, you must," she said taking his damp hand and placing it on her breast.

His heart pounded as she led him through the door and into her bed chamber.

"But, you did it because it was ordained," Suffi said holding his hand as they lay side by side in his bed. "You have loved her all your life and she has loved you. It was destined to happen."

"I feel I have betrayed you by sleeping with her."

"No, my love. You could never betray me. You are a good man and came to me at once to tell me what you did. I don't fear her. I know you love me and our child. It is the way of my people and the gods. Being with your sister is not forbidden in my land. You must think of my approval as your abiding by a custom of Thebes. You have my everlasting love but I will not stand in your way if you wish to return to her bed."

"Suffi. Suffi, where did I ever find such a wonderful and understanding woman?"

"Feel the little one jump. He is excited about meeting his father."

Akhu wrapped her in his arms and closed his eyes wishing the vision of Sabra would go away.

But, it was not to be. The smell of her, the feel of Sabra's soft skin, her breath mingled with his, intoxicated him day and night. Though he tried, a distancing began between Suffi and him.

Many nights he didn't share Suffi's bed and was gone until dawn. He couldn't understand how she would just smile and open her arms for him as he came into the room smelling of Sabra's oils and sweat, as a new day lightened the sky overhead. No matter how he tried, he couldn't understand the unusual customs of her land, those of Thebes where the distinction between man and woman was blurred and coupling between friends was the norm. Egypt had its openness between the sexes but nothing like the ways of Thebes.

Suffi, warmed by her love for Akhu, grew and grew, the baby swelling her body yet never diminishing her beauty.

Akhu was summoned to the palace where he stood below the raised platform, close to where Sabra sat at the pharaoh's feet.

King Nebrunef rested on his throne, a maid fanning his immense body, another bathing his feet in aromatic oils.

One hundred of his family and staff were assembled in the throne room as the pharaoh surveyed the mass of people in front of him, his hand running up and down the gold snake of authority coiled on his arm. The Ankh fertility symbol lay in his lap.

All were silent, each one knowing something important was about to be uttered by their god.

Sabra, her hand resting on the pharaoh's foot, chanced a glance at Akhu who lowered his head and looked at the tiled floor so his expression would not give them away.

A staff, wrapped on the tile by a priest, brought the room to absolute silence.

"I will die before the egrets return from the sea," the pharaoh said to the silent room. "The after-life awaits me and all of us. I have been told by the Librarian that the tomb is almost finished. It is your King's wish that I be entombed, as has been the custom for twenty dynasties, and travel to the golden land to sit beside the gods."

No one moved a muscle, some knowing what was coming, others stunned by what their living god had said.

"As your Pharaoh, I look for the last time on my family and servants. Isis comes for me and for you. Be joyous. We will travel the river together and live forever in peace and harmony."

A murmur rose from the crowd but no one spoke out loud.

King Nebrunef reached and took Queen Paqui's hand in his. She smiled but it faded when her king reached down with his other hand and took Sabra's.

"On either side of my sarcophagus will be those of my queen and my favorite consort."

Akhu's head snapped up when he realized what the king was saying. All his relatives, slaves, and consorts, his entire court would be killed and buried in the tomb that he had designed and worked on so hard to finish. All, including his beloved sister, Sabra, would be buried in a tomb that would be sealed, each person mummified for the journey to what some called heaven.

Though no one else noticed, a tear slid down Sabra's cheek.

Sabra lay on her bed, oiled and perfumed, naked but for a thin sheet across her lap. Her maid, Juji, stood by her door, her ear to the wood panel, listening.

"He comes," she said opening it a bit and peering out.

Akhu slipped inside the room and walked to the side of her bed. Looking down at Sabra, he smiled and touched her arm.

"You look sad. That is no way to greet your love," Akhu said.

"Of course I am sad. Aren't you? He has just told us we will all be killed and I am to be buried next to his sarcophagus, his ugly wife on the other side."

"I will not let it happen."

"Ha! A librarian who will defy the Pharaoh?"

He smiled and dropped his tunic to the floor, the maid, Juji, picking it up as he crawled into bed beside Sabra.

"I will get the best in the land to help us," Akhu cried holding the blackness of Suffi in his arms, her face contorted, tears running down her cheeks. "You must fight and live."

"There is nothing I can do. The child is not moving. The priests say he is too big and is dead. I fear I will not survive."

He held her tightly and cried into her long, dark hair.

"My love, my love. What will I do without you?"

"You will take your sister away. Leave this place and make a new life somewhere with her. I will look down and guide you no matter where you go."

"You must not die. It can be expelled. I will talk to the surgeon."

"I have already spoken to him. The child is dead. Removing him with a knife will kill me just as certainly as if we wait for the gods to take me."

"But we must try. I cannot let this happen."

Two days later, Suffi lay in a pool of blood, the surgeon standing over her with a sharp, bloody knife in his hand, a sad expression on his face.

"I tried as you commanded but the child was too big. She is gone. I am sorry."

Akhu held her limp tattooed hand and cried at the loss of his son and the woman who had been by his side as a slave and a lover, a woman more loyal than any he had ever met, and now she was gone.

He stared down into Suffi's face, eyes closed, yet looking so alive. Solemnly, he remembered her last words, that he should take Sabra and leave before the command was given for them all to be killed and prepared for entombment in the temple.

But Sabra refused to leave saying her god had decided what was best for all of those who worshiped him, his order to be obeyed that his court would travel to the after-world and continue to serve him.

"I am sorry but this is how it must be," she had said.

Akhu, however, refused to give up.

His days of mourning for Suffi passed slowly. Akhu buried himself in work, completing the job of overseeing the temple's construction and retuning each night after dark, eating a small meal, and retiring alone to his bed pad. Over and over, he thought of the brave, black woman who had shared so many trials and adventures with him and marveled at how open and loyal and wonderful she had been, a friend, a lover, a fighter, beautiful, and brave until the very end.

Twice, he was summoned by Sabra's maid to come to the palace and be with her. Twice he obeyed and was swept away from his grief in her arms.

The head priest gave ominous warnings to the Pharaoh, warnings of trumpet calls from the god, Usiris, calls summoning him. A weak man, King Nebrunef worried himself into a weakened state of mind and body. No matter how his attendants insisted, he refused to eat, taking only one meal a day of bread and beer plus the medicine Queen Paqui laddeled out for him..

Sabra watched her huge king wither away and soon become bed ridden. He called for her a few times but his body would not respond and she was allowed to return to the concubine's quarters.

Though Sabra grieved for her pharaoh, Queen Paqui became more outgoing and decisive than ever. She ignored the poor state of his health and took upon herself many of the Pharaoh's duties. Sabra, as part of the inner court, watched and suspected the woman was planning on being King Nebrunef's successor, the eleventh queen of the twenty seven dynasties.

One night, as Akhu lay in her arms, Sabra leaned back on her pillows.

"Do you think our king is being poisoned?" she asked.

"Impossible. Who would do such a thing?"

"The queen. Have you not noticed how she is taking over now that he is bedridden and not functioning?"

"Yes, but why..."

"She wishes to be the next pharaoh. As the successor to our king, she will be spared the death that awaits the rest of the court."

"If this is true, there is still nothing anyone can do about it." Akhu said in a resigned voice.

"I am not so sure. Please be ready for anything. I will..."

There was a loud shout in the outer hall and Sabra's maid, Juji, burst into the room.

"Mistress, one of the Queen's people saw Master Akhu enter your chambers. I have sent someone to stop him but I worry if she finds out that you are with someone other than our king?"

Sabra looked at Akhu and said, "It has begun. Be very careful who you trust."

With that she got up. Juji pulled a gown over her, and Sabra went to the window.

"You had best leave, my Akhu. Take care."

"But..."

"I will be safe. Please do not worry."

Chapter Eighteen - The Conspiracy

Akhu rushed from Sabra's quarters and made his way back to the Library only to find men rushing about frantically.

"What is happening?" he asked one of the head scribes.

"Word of the Romans has arrived. Two Legions approach the city. We are being surrounded. I fear we will starve to death or die at the end of a Roman sword."

"How much time do we have?"

"We think days, maybe a week."

Akhu ran his hand through his hair, thinking, trying to figure out what to do. There were over

700,000 scrolls in the Library and he knew what the Romans thought about such things.

"We must remove the scrolls and hide them," Akhu said in a low voice. "Gather all you can trust. We will take them to the Kings tomb. I know a chamber where they will be safe."

"The Pharaoh's tomb?" the scribe whispered. "But, it is sacred."

"Do as I say and move quickly."

For the next two days, under the cover of darkness, a steady column of men moved from the Library out to the Tomb of King Nebrunef. All night they made the dangerous journey through the city and out into the desert wasteland where the tomb rose up in a starlit sky in the Valley of the Dead.

Sabra was advised by Akhu of what was happening and drew a deep sigh. She knew what must be done and gave the order to her personal guard that all of the men who assisted Akhu be killed so the whereabouts of the scrolls would be known only to a few.

Akhu mourned the death of his fellow conspirators but understood and reluctantly agreed.. Thirty men died in their sleep the following night.

Sabra summoned Akhu to her rooms.

"Our king grows weaker by the moment and I fear his death is imminent. The queen will make her move the moment he dies. She will live but I and all the court will die and be entombed with the Pharaoh forever."

"Is that still what you wish, to lie with your pharaoh?"

"I have a great conflict about it and don't know what to do. Please listen careful because there is something I must tell you."

"You look worried. It is not like you," Akhu said as she took his hand.

"Place your palm here," she said moving it onto her bare belly.

"Your skin is warm and wonderful as always."

"You are not felling deeply enough, my Akhu. There is a little one in there."

He pulled his hand away which she placed back and covered with hers.

"This child may be the answer. The priests have touched me as you are doing and tell me it is a boy child."

"Do you think the king will change his mind if he knows he has an heir?"

"The child you feel is not his, Akhu. It is yours. The King has not been with me since he has become sick, too long for him to be the father."

"But you have gone to his chambers often. You have told me so."

"He is no longer a man. I did whatever I knew but could not raise him. You are the father, not the king."

Akhu looked stunned, his mind reeling with the implications. Once before he had faced the idea of having a child when Suffi had held his hand in the same way against her black belly. But, she had died along with his son. Now Sabra, his great love, was telling him he would soon become a father. But she was the king's consort, second only to the queen. What if his spies or the priests figured out that it was impossible for this child to be his heir. Once doubt took hold, Sabra would be killed at once.

An idea flashed into his mind like a whirlwind

"How loyal are your people?"

"You mean those that serve the second consort? They are absolutely loyal."

"Some know of my visits," he said.

Sabra smiled at Juji, her maid, standing in the shadows.

"Only Juji knows and she would die before speaking of you."

"Is she loyal enough to risk a torturous death if we fail?" he said then whispered, "Loyal enough to stand by you when you summon the priests and demand that you be declared Pharaoh as the mother of his heir?"

"Do not make fun of me."

"What if we presented you to the priests, assure them that you carry the heir to their king. It is custom for the mother to stand as Pharaoh until the child is old enough to assume the throne. You are smarter than the queen, younger, from a royal family, loyal to the gods. They know how the queen wants to replace Isis and Horus with her own god. Would they listen and back you as their new pharaoh?"

"By Isis, you are serious."

"I am. You would become a god and be worshiped by all of Egypt."

"But, the Romans who surround our city will not let that happen. They will come and burn Alexandria to the ground."

"So there are a number of choices. We die at the hands of the King's guard and be entombed with him. Or, we stand up to the queen and make you our next Pharaoh. Or, we wait for the Romans to decide for us. The choice is easy for me. I will serve you to my death."

"Do you think the Romans would back away if they knew there was a new and possibly more co-operative Pharaoh?"

"It is their pattern," Akhu said. "They prefer to set up friendly governments than to occupy far off lands. It could work."

"May I count on you to make this offer to the Romans?"

"I will go at once."

She reached over and took his face in her hands and kissed him on the mouth.

"Who would have believed when we were children that someday your sister would be the next Pharaoh?"

"I've always believed in you."

She smiled and walked with him to the door.

"Come to me the moment you return. In the meantime, I will think on this grand scheme of yours."

Akhu, dressed in his most formal tunic, left the city under the cover of darkness, alone and unarmed. Beneath his tunic he carried a small scroll from Sabra to the commander of the Roman Legions.

At the edge of the Roman camp, he was stopped and made to explain his reason for walking into an armed, enemy position. Convincing the guards of his mission, he was brought to a mid-level Centurion and spent an hour explaining his purpose. Again, he was forceful and presented a strong case and was led to the Roman Prefect, a noble from Rome itself.

"I have been told of your scheme to save Alexandria," the man said looking up from his field desk.

"Sir, I have long felt that too many good men die in wars when it is almost never necessary. Thousands will die in an attack against Alexandria and the city will be destroyed. What if you had a sympathetic Pharaoh who ran Egypt as a friend of Rome. Trade and learning would flourish. History would look upon those who made such a decision as great men. I have in my hand a scroll from the only woman who can do this."

"What of the Pharaoh and his Queen. Are they not able to do as you suggest?"

"Ask your scouts. The Pharaoh is very sick. The queen is scheming to become Pharaoh herself and has said openly that no one can defeat Egypt's armies. Together, we can save many lives and also the city of Alexandria and its great treasures."

The Prefect looked long and hard at this young man who had come with such a daring plan.

"What would you need from me?"

"A promise to allow the woman who wrote this scroll to live and prosper as a friend of Rome."

"That is all?"

"Yes. We will do what has to be done among ourselves if you hold off your invasion until you hear from me again."

"You are a very brave man, Master Akhu. I will grant you twelve days until the feast of Zeus. We will wait. If you come to me successful, we will sit with your new Queen and make a peaceful agreement."

Akhu bowed and backed out of the Prefect's presence.

"Wonderful," she said, "But how do we proceed.?"

"You must have an audience with the high priest. He is an ambitious man and will hopefully listen to you."

"And the Romans have given you only twelve days to arrange all this?"

"Yes," he said and smiled at her. "You will be the most beautiful pharaoh Egypt has ever seen.

She took Akhu in her arms and pressed her growing belly against him.

"Though he is unborn, I sense a great leader in him. Do you feel his frantic efforts to come out and govern our sacred land?"

Sabra made sure she sat in a dominant position, a throne-like carved wooden chair, her bare arms resting on a pair of lavishly painted lion's heads. Her gown was of the thinnest linen streaked with gold thread and intentionally left open to show her bare, swollen belly.

Standing in front of Sabra was the high priest along with others who represented the gods, Isis and Horus, three men in all black, stern, and wicked looking to her eyes.

"I have called you as a decision must be made soon. The king has only a few days left and grows weaker by the minute. We must make plans for his sacred journey."

The priests nodded, still stunned by her announcement of the king's child in her belly. It had been her intention to shock them with the news and move quickly toward her solution for when the king died.

"Queen Paqui has already instructed us," the high priest said more to his assistants than to her. "On the day of his death, those on the list will be executed and made ready for entombment."

The priest of Horus looked uncomfortable. He of all the priests knew the queen would honor her favorite god, Sobek, the crocodile god, in place of all others.

"What bothers you, priest?" Sabra asked.

"I do not speak against Queen Paqui but there may be another solution. You carry the king's boy heir. It is evident he will be born soon. Should he not live to see his kingdom?"

The high priest glared at him and turned to face Sabra again.

"The orders have been given by Pharaoh himself. Your sarcophagus has been cast and awaits in the tomb. The feasts have been prepared. The Kings death mask is all that remains before he is embalmed and placed with his heart in the burial coffin."

"Has the king been told he has an heir?" the young priest asked.

"No. he is too weak and cannot understand. He should not be bothered," the high priest said..

"I will tell him at once and we will be advised by him as to how to proceed." Sabra said in a commanding voice. "He is our Pharaoh and we will obey his commands until he departs for the afterworld."

"Yes, Mistress," the high priest said turning and leaving, his face flushed with anger.

"He will cause much mischief," Sabra said to Akhu. "The priest is on the Queen's side and will do whatever he can to make her Pharaoh."

"You look very beautiful," Akhu said running his eyes over Sabra who stood before a reflecting metal disk, her hands cupping her swollen stomach.

"Beautiful enough to convince a dying man?"

"Yes, and all Egypt will follow you. Good luck."

Her maid, Juji, draped a cloak around Sabra's shoulders and smiled as her mistress walked down the long hallway to the king's chambers.

Sabra hesitated for a moment then tapped on the massive door and was admitted by a young maid who attended his needs.

"I come before my King," Sabra said walking over to his canopied bed.

He lay on damp sheets, his once huge body shriveled from dysentery and pain. His hand reached out which she took and kneeled by the bed.

"Are you feeling better on this beautiful day?" she asked in a low voice.

"I have great pain and will make my journey soon."

"Do not say that. I need you. We need you."

His hand reached out and rested on the swollen mound of her belly.

"A child. You are with child?"

"Yes, my dear one. We are having a boy child. The priests have told me it will be a male."

"A boy? An heir to the kingdom? By Isis woman, why have you not told me this before?"

"I have. I have told you many times but it is easy to forget when you are in such pain."

"He will lead the twenty-eighth dynasty. My son. May the gods be praised. He will be called Thet and be a great king."

"But that will not be so if you die and we, your son and I, travel to the afterworld with you."

The king ran his hand round and round her belly.

"I feel my son move." he said smiling. "With all my wives and slaves, no one has given me an heir. Too many were born dead, too many females, too many deceits. But, you kneel there and offer me a son?"

"It is my life I give you, my king."

"Guard!" he shouted at the top of his weak lungs.

The door swung open and an armed man rushed to his side.

"Bring the priests, my queen, and the librarian to note what I have to say. I have an announcement to make."

She kneeled by the bed, holding his hand for what seemed like an endless five minutes until Akhu, the high priest, his two assistants, and Queen Paqui arrived all looking worried and nervous.

Still holding Sabra's hand, he looked up at them and smiled.

"Soon I will depart this world and desire for you to listen carefully."

"Please, my love, do not strain yourself," the queen whispered. "Take your medicine. We will wait outside."

"No. I will speak and you will listen."

He reached over and lay his hand on Sabra's belly.

"My son, Thet, waits for the light of day." he looked into Sabra's damp eyes. "You will be Queen Regent until Thet's eighth birthday when he will be coronated as Pharaoh. As Queen Regent you will be Pharaoh until then. These are my commands."

The queen went pale. The high priest lowered his eyes then looked at Sabra with venom. Akhu said nothing just noted on a scroll what was said and handed it to the pharaoh who read it with great effort. Akhu handed him the official stamp which he laboriously pressed into hot wax and sealed his pronouncement.

Sabra stood and looked at the Queen with narrowed eyes.

"Please hand me the medicine. I wish to have it examined by the King's doctors."

The queen pressed it to her chest, nodding her head no.

"You will hand it to me at once," Sabra said in a deep, resonant voice that echoed off the walls of the king's chambers.

A guard took the vial from the queen's trembling hands. Everyone in the room stared at Sabra who faced them, her massive belly parting her linen gown.

She put her hands on her belly and looked from one to the other.

"You will hear the thoughts of your new Pharaoh, Thet, from my mouth. I will be your

Queen from this day forward and rule Egypt wisely. All who feel otherwise will be dealt with as Isis desires. Now, kneel and give me your allegiance."

Everyone but Queen Paqui dropped to their knees. She bit her lip, turned, and left the king's chambers as quickly as her feet could move.

Akhu, on his knees, swore his life to his love, the new Pharaoh. The high priest mumbled yet did her bidding.

"Now, I would spend the Kings last hours by his side." she said looking at Akhu. "Please announce the ascension to the people. Tell them about the King's heir and their new queen."

All of them backed out of the chambers leaving Sabra alone with the king.

"You did well, my queen," the old man said in a near whisper. "How I wish I was able to thank you in a proper way."

"You have. You have made your son and me very happy. We will be wise and rule as you have. I will make your journey to the After Life the best any pharaoh has ever experienced."

He smiled and closed his eyes.

"No one questioned the paternity of the child?" Akhu said sitting on a pillow near where Sabra lay, her hands on her belly, her eyes on the ceiling.

"No one knew that the king has been impotent for months, that is no one but the queen. But, she was so rattled by the idea that the medicine she's been forcing into his mouth was poison, that she missed her chance. But, I must move quickly. There is much to do to be sure the army is with me and that the palace guard will be loyal as well."

"I have spoken to the guard," Akhu said. "They will be at your side. The queen, unfortunately, has great influence with the army and will cause trouble but there are good men who are your generals. They will listen if you explain our plan of how to deal with the Romans."

"Please arrange a meeting at once with General Phet."

The man stepped through the doorway to the king's chambers dressed in his finest battle clothes and armor. He was alone as had been requested.

Akhu met him the moment he entered the hallway, nodded his greeting, and led the old warrior toward the king's bed chamber.

"I worry that this will be too much for him," the general said to Akhu. "Can we not meet elsewhere?"

"No. I have been instructed by the Queen Regent that you must have an audience with the king."

"So be it."

They entered the bedroom. Sabra was again kneeling by his bedside holding his fevered hand but turned when they entered.

"My king, your General Phet approaches. He wishes to hear your voice and your wisdom."

The general came close to the bed, obviously nervous being in the presence of the Pharaoh and seeing him in such poor shape.

"My King," he said kneeling.

She brought his hand over and lay it on top of the general's.

"I wish for you to listen to Queen Sabra," the dying man said. "She is my voice. Do as she instructs and all will be well."

The general turned to her, his face flushed with surprise.

"Queen Sabra? Where, if I may be so bold to ask, is Queen Paqui?"

"She has been deposed by your king," Sabra said. "She has failed him in many ways and will be punished. I carry the king's boy child, Thet, who will be your Pharaoh in eight years. Until then, I am your queen regent and pharaoh."

She looked at the king and said, "Is that not so, my king?"

"It is so," he croaked in a weak voice.

The general, totally confused, looked back and forth between them, finally bowing his head to her and saying, "My queen."

"I wish for you to stand and listen to me carefully."

He rose from his kneeling position and stood at attention by the bedside.

"My King will not live through the night. Our child was announced to the priests and the king has signed a document naming his son, Thet, the new pharaoh and me as regent until he is eight years old. Do you understand this?"

"Yes, it is as the pharaoh said."

She stood and came close to him.

"There are four legions of Roman soldiers camped a few days from Alexandria. Can your army defeat them?"

"The general looked at his sandals and took a deep breath.

"We do not have the troops to defeat such a force. So much of the treasury has gone to the construction of the tomb that I have fewer than five thousand men to defend Alexandria."

"You are wise to have told me this," she said. "Now, what if I told you there may not be a need to fight. Five thousand of my bravest men will live to see another day."

"If it could only be so?"

"The librarian has met with their Prefect and has received a promise that they will not attack for another six days but after that, they swear not a building or soul will be left standing in Alexandria."

"What do they want in return?"

"They wish only to trade and see us prosper within their orbit and not the Greeks who have all but left us on our own."

"But..."

"Do you doubt I can do this?" Sabra asked in a loud voice.

"No. No. I just..."

"To accomplish this I need the loyalty of you and your army of five thousand. If we succeed in holding the Romans at bay, I will reward each man five gold coins."

"The men will follow you to the end of the earth for such a sum."

"And, do I have your loyalty as well?"

The general, not one to make quick decisions, spent a long moment reviewing all she had said plus the promises Queen Paqui had made to him only hours before.

"The army will be yours to command," he said bowing his head to her.

"Do you trust him?" Akhu asked. "We only have six days."

"I must. But the ex-queen is conspiring against me. I know it."

"You have the king's document making you Regent. You have the priests out of the picture and away from the king. You have the guard on your side, and the promise of the general. I would say you have done well."

"But, only as long as our pharaoh lives. When he dies, we shall see who is with who?"

.

Chapter Nineteen - The Entombment

She was at his side when Pharaoh Nebrunef drew his last breath. The palace, though prepared for his death, fell into deep mourning. As the word spread throughout the countryside, all of Egypt collapsed into darkness. The passing of a pharaoh was a huge event looked on as a monumental calling from the gods.

The tomb was finished, even the pair of cast bronze sarcophagus for ex-queen Paqui and Sabra, his consort, coffin-like boxes already beside the pharaoh's final resting place. Tables of food and many of his favorite possessions, gold and jewelry, were sent to the tomb while a death mask was taken from his face and cast in bronze to be placed on the metal statue on top of his sarcophagus.

With his death came a new dynamic. Ignoring, the ascension of Sabra, the priests moved quickly to solidify their command of the burial ceremony. While Sabra mourned in her chambers, all relatives of the kings, his concubines, his slaves, even his marginally sane brother, were assembled in the palace and brought before the high priest.

With Queen Paqui by his side, the high priest announced that the killings would begin the following morning and, after being embalmed, a parade of chariots carrying the death attendants would be taken to the tomb and locked up for eternity beside their dead pharaoh.

The family, the king's servants, and slaves bowed their heads, accepting their fate as the gods had decreed.

A young priest came to the high priest, his hands bloody and holding the King's heart. It was weighed and found light and worthy. With great ceremony the heart was placed back in his empty chest, the only organ left in his body. His heart would keep him well on his journey to the afterworld.

Though Sabra had the scroll that made her position as the regent clear, Queen Paqui and the high priest inflamed everyone who would listen saying Sabra was an imposter and she should be held to the king's original burial orders and buried beside him. They made the case that the Pharaoh was not of his right mind when he made her Regent and the unborn child, the next pharaoh.

The generals listened and gave way to Queen Paqui's demands. The guard stayed loyal but knew they must be silent or they would all be killed.

The high priest came to Sabra's chambers on the third day after his death.

"It is time," he said standing in her doorway not stepping inside for fear of her maid, Juji, who stood in front of Sabra with a drawn dagger in her hand.

Word had reached her of the traitorous plans of the ex-queen and the high priest. Sabra looked at him with an expression of resignation on her lovely face and stepped around her maid, telling her it was useless. She looked at him for a moment, then doubled up in pain, dropping to her knees on the floor, a river of water flowing down her legs.

"Pharaoh Thet is here," Juji shouted at the top of her lungs.

People from all over the palace came running, swept Sabra up, and took her to her bed.

Within an hour, Thet was born, a perfect child with curly, black hair not unlike that of the librarian.

Akhu raced into the room, and dropped to the side of her bed. She smiled and showed him the child.

"He is as lovely and as beautiful as you are," she whispered.

Akhu, not caring who saw, kissed her hand and wept.

""The rumor is true," Queen Paqui's eunuch whispered to her. "It is not the king's child."

"But there is no way to prove it, you fool," she screamed. "Get out of my sight."

The ex-queen lay back on her pillows. All was ruined. If the stupid priest had only killed Sabra first and not hesitated, the outcome would be as it should have been. But no, he insisted on making her the last to be killed so she would suffer seeing all her friends and servants die.

"What am I going to do?" she said to the cat curled up on the foot of her bed.

One of the jars of poison sat on her table. She looked at it for a long time wondering how she could get Sabra to take it then threw it on the floor where the jar broke into a hundred pieces.

"She and that bastard child must die," she said picking up a small idol of her private god, Sobek, the crocodile. "Give me the strength, my pretty god."

She knew the risk. If it was not done properly, she would lose her life in a most horrible way. But, she was to die anyway as the queen of her dead pharaoh and spend eternity at his side.

"How can they be killed? I can trust no one for this. I must do it myself," she whispered to the cat, "And what greater pleasure than bringing death to that evil girl who dares to take my throne?"

A knock on the door came disrupting her thoughts as a maid let the high priest into her chambers. He stood by the window looking out.

"If this entombment of the king does not proceed as planned, you and I are at great risk, Queen Paqui," he said.

"What are you saying? Am I not condemned to be killed and placed at his side?"

"If there is no regent or no child pharaoh, who else can rule this land?"

She smiled, just what she had been thinking. Kill the usurper and her bastard child.

"What if we tell the important people that the child is not the king's rightful heir?"

"No one will believe that. They must die and you must do it," he said turning to face her. "You are the only one who can get close to her. She will not allow me in her presence."

"What if I go to her and tell her I am willing to make peace."

"Then you will be pharaoh and we can put all this to rest."

Chapter Twenty - Sabra's Death

"Mistress, Queen Paqui stands in the hallway with a peace offering in her hand," Juji said. "She lies but tells me she wishes for nothing but harmony between the two of you."

Sabra looked up from watching tiny Thet sucking at her breast.

"Show her in, Juji."

"But, she is filled with evil. I do not trust her."

"All is changed now that Thet is born and she recognizes that this beautiful child is the heir and I am Regent. Let her in," Sabra said shifting the baby to her other breast.

As exquisite as she had ever been, Sabra leaned back on the mound of pillows and waited, her child nestled in her arm, her young body naked to the waist, olive toned skin glistening from the aromatic oils spread on her by faithful, Juji.

"Queen Paqui," Juji announced from the doorway and stepped aside.

"So this is our new Pharaoh," the woman said entering the bed chamber. "He is as beautiful as they say but has such dark hair."

Sabra smiled and looked down at her child.

"Why have you come?" she said looking up at the stern face of the ex-queen.

"I have come to make peace. There is no need for such animosity in the hours before my death. I wish to go to the tomb as a woman who has become a friend to the Regent and of the boy pharaoh."

Juji coughed from the shadows.

"Is this true?"

"I swear by Isis that I speak the truth."

The queen reached out with her hand and touched the child's puffy cheek.

"He grows fat on your rich milk," she said in a soft voice.

Sabra smiled and looked down at her baby. As she gazed at her child, a scream came from Juji. A man in black held a knife to her throat.

Queen Paqui stepped closer and drew a dagger from inside her toga.

"Look at my face, imposter. I am the queen and will be Pharaoh when you die. Look at me not at this bastard child. I know who impregnated you and it was not that stupid man I endured for so many years."

The women's eyes met for a moment before Queen Paqui's arm rose high and her dagger plunged into Sabra's heart. She withdrew it slowly and drove it again and again deep into the young Regent's body.

Covered with blood, the ex-queen, picked up the baby and threw it at the wall. A loud thud, and the boy pharaoh fell to the floor lifeless.

Juji lay on the floor, unconscious, spared by the man in black who had defied the ex-queen and not choked her to death as he had been ordered.

Akhu lay on his bed pad, awake but still groggy from sleep. A pounding on his door brought him around. Quickly, he stumbled to the latch and peered out to see the frightened face of Juji.

"The queen has killed them. You must flee at once. They are coming for you."

"Dead! My Sabra! Why? Why?"

"Quickly. I hear them."

Akhu, trusting Juji, but totally confused by what she had said, grabbed his sword, and tucked his pouch into the waistband of his sleeping garment, took her by the hand, and fled the library.

She led him to a passageway that burrowed under the wall, a secret tunnel that only the innermost people of the palace knew existed, helped him push a covering panel aside, and dragged a dazed Akhu into darkness.

They stumbled along the damp, narrow tunnel for what seemed like forever until they came to some steps leading up. He put his shoulders to a stone and the two of them burst out into fresh air and escape.

She had told him what happened as they raced through the tunnel but his mind was reeling with sorrow and guilt.

"I can't believe this. Are you positive they are dead?"

"The witch stabbed her so many times. No one could have lived through that and the child, Oh, the child. His head was ...."

"She will be pharaoh and will hunt us no matter where we go," Akhu said, the magnitude of it all finally soaking in. "We must make it to the desert where we can disappear."

Chapter Twenty One - Juji's Tribe

They mounted a hill overlooking Alexandria and turned one last time to see their beloved city.

"What is happening?" she shouted as they stared at the city below.

Flames leaped high in the air as building after building was consumed by fire.

Akhu sighed and sat at her feet, his hands covering his face and wept. It was the twelfth day, the day of Zeus, the end of the truce with the Romans. Two Legions had attacked and the city of Alexandria was in flames.

They stood in the darkness on the hillside and watched as section after section of the city burned sending flames crackling into the air, the sounds of terror from unseen voices. An explosion racked the night and his tears continued to flow as the Mouseion, his beloved library, burned, thousands of scrolls still inside, gone, knowledge lost forever to mankind.

"Why is Isis punishing me? Why did he have her killed? What have I done?" he cried out in anguish then, after watching the inferno below, turned to Juji. "The only good thing I did was bury many of the scrolls with the dead king. Some day they may see the light of day again."

Juji handed him the scroll naming dead Thet as pharaoh. Akhu rolled it in his fingers.

"Sabra was pharaoh for ten days. Will anyone ever know?"

"You must flee with me to the desert and find a way to tell the world."

She took his hand as they turned their backs on the burning city of Alexandria and stepped into the sands of Egypt, away from the fertile Nile and into the unknown.

The two of them staggered through the sand, struggling up one dune and down another without water, Akhu walking ahead, his bed clothes ripped and torn, Juji in her sleeping garment, their skin bared to a merciless Egyptian sun. Tears took precious water from Akhu's body ass he continued to weep for his sister, Sabra, the mother of his child, the woman who had been at his side from the time they had learned to walk, a loss that would never heal.

Juji, walking beside him, understood his grief having been so close to Sabra, probably her best friend though she was a mere slave and only a maid to the consort. Her bare feet burned from the hot sand, her shoulders red from the rays pounding down from above but nothing pained as much as how her heart felt. She would miss Sabra in a different way. She had shared so much of her mistresses' life. As a good and trusted slave, she had been in the shadows at all times, guarded her, pampered her, watched as Sabra and Akhu made love, listened as they had plotted her ascension to the throne, and shared Sabra's confidences and fears. Looking almost like twins, they had shared clothes and made each other up with kohl and henna, played with hair styles, and revealed secrets. Not only identical in appearance, they even thought the same way. If anyone knew Sabra as well as Akhu, it was Juji.

"Where are you taking us?" Akhu asked as the sun faded and a cooler night descended.

"My tribe is but a day away. We will go there to hide from those who will come looking for us."

She found a small plant in the shadow of a stone, plucked it and broke it in two. A drop of water fell into her palm which she held out for Akhu.

"Drink from my palm. I will find another as we walk."

He took her hand in his and touched his tongue to her warm hand, licked the pearl-like drop from her palm, and smiled.

"If I was not so dazed by the sun, I would think I had just kissed the hand of our Sabra."

She smiled and said, "If that were only so."

Exhausted, and nearly dead from thirst, they staggered into the Bedouin camp deep in the desert. Friendly hands, carried them to shelter, bathed and fed them, and made them sleep.

A day later, Akhu woke to look into the eyes of Sabra. He reached out to touch her, startled at the sight of his dead sister, and grasped the hand of Juji.

"It is I, Juji. Do not look so startled."

"I thought it was...."

"It is only me. Here, take a sip from this cup."

She held a warm bowl to his lips and helped him drink.

"Another few hours in the desert and we would not have made it here," she said holding it for him to drink again.

"How did you know where they were?"

She smiled.

"My family has made the same trek every year since the beginning of time. It is early fall. I knew they would be here at the oasis before it dries up during the months to come."

"Are we safe from those who look for us?"

"They would not dream of our coming this far into the western desert. No one but we nomads come here. There is nothing, no cities, very little water, nothing. Why would they look here?"

"A smart man would wonder where we might go to be safe? Where no one else lives might be a thought that passes through his mind."

She smiled again.

"A hundred armed nomads will be a match for any intruder. Do not worry so much."

He lay back and sighed as Juji bustled about picking up discarded clothing, a chamber pot, a soiled pillow. His eyes watered as he watched this vision move about. It was as if his Sabra walked in her sandals.

"It is amazing how much you look like her," he said.

"She chose me from many candidates. It was her idea to have me stand in for her when she did not want to attend some gathering or another, or did not want the affection of the king..."

"You replaced her with the King and he never knew?"

Juji smiled and nodded yes.

"Amazing, just amazing."

A month passed as their strength returned. Juji resumed her role as one of the leaders of her tribe and sat with the elders at their meetings. Her young sister, Janis, stayed constantly by her side. Akhu, however, feel into fits of depression often, refusing to eat or leave his small tent. Days would go by as he lay on his pad staring at the tent poles above, not speaking or moving, a silent ghost of the learned man he had been. Then, as suddenly as the depression came, it vanished and he left the tent and ate like three men, even joined them around the fire at night.

It was at one of these nightly gatherings that news arrived about Alexandria. A slave from the palace had escaped after the great fire when all was in chaos.

"Tell me what is happening in the city," Akhu asked.

"I can only repeat what these ears overheard. I am sorry to tell you that the Mouseion, the library, has been gutted by the Romans who have no use for foreign knowledge. The city is slowly recovering but none of the remaining treasure is meant for a rebuilding of the library. I am afraid all is lost."

"Who is the king? Who is running the city, the Roman Prefect?"

"No. The new pharaoh is the old one's brother."

"The half-wit? Why he can barely write." Akhu said in amazement.

"He is but a figure head. The real power rests with the high priest who has taken over everything."

"What of Queen Pique?"

"She and the second consort rest for all time next to King Nebrunef in the tomb. It was done while the city still burned. She was killed along with the servants and slaves. All were sent to the tomb to be beside the king forever."

Akhu dropped his cup and bit at his lip, the vision of his Sabra entombed alongside the queen made his stomach churn.

"What of the Romans?" he said when he'd regained his composure.

"The Prefect has given the high priest full governing powers as long as Egypt pays a handsome tribute and enters into trade with Rome rather than with the Greeks."

"So the priest sits where Sabra should be. If I live to be one hundred years old, I will rectify this injustice."

The tribe moved at the prescribed time, packed up all their tents and possessions. On horseback and camel they traveled toward the sea but still in the Western desert. Days went by without seeing another living soul.

"We near the beach," Juji said riding up beside him. "Our place is there." she said pointing from a hill top toward a lush valley beside one of the small tributaries of the Nile, a narrow stream meandering toward the sea, its brown silt marking the blue Mediterranean.

"It has rich ground from the floods, fresh water, and fruit trees. Do you like it?"

"It is quite beautiful but why not stay here all year rather than roam the dry, hot desert?'

She looked at him with surprise then smiled when her younger sister, Janis spoke up.

"It is our way and has been for centuries," the young girl said.

"Let us move quickly so I can show you before it gets dark." Juji said.

They spurred their horses and galloped down the hillside toward the sea.

"You ride well," he shouted.

She galloped beside him, her long, black hair flying like a banner, her thin dress pressed tight against her body, bare knees squeezing into the steed's ribs urging him to run faster, a vision he likened to his Sabra

On down the slope they rode, across fertile, flat land, and along the banks of the river they had seen from above, the horses eager with the smell of the sea in their flaring nostrils. They galloped as fast as the steeds would go until they came to a small cliff overlooking the water. Juji pulled back on the reins and looked down. Slowly, she urged her horse to step carefully but surely onto the gentle slope that led to a white beach. Down and onto the sand they slipped and slid, the horses snorting and rearing at the sound of the surf.

"Easy, girl," Juji said patting the mare's neck. "Let's cool you off?"

She led her horse into the shallows, urging it forward with her knees and a soothing voice. Once the horses were quieted and walking slowly through knee deep water, she turned to Akhu and cried out, "Ha. Ha," and jabbed her knees into her mare's ribs.

The horse bolted forward, charging through the surf with Akhu right beside her.

Never had he felt such a wonderful thrill as charging along the beach, horses splashing water high with their hoofs, a sea breeze in his face, and the sight of a gorgeous woman racing by his side.

"Like it?" she shouted.

"It is wonderful. I could do this forever."

She smiled, happy that she had found a way to relieve his misery.

"The small, fresh water creek is just ahead where we can water the horses," she said racing out in front of him.

Water tumbled down the cliff side from some unknown source above, ran along a pebbled creek bed a couple of arms lengths wide, and poured into the sea. She jumped off her horse and led it to the creek where it drank as she patted its side.

"We will let them drink and nibble on this fresh grass. Come. I will show you a place of my childhood."

She took his hand and led him through knee deep water around a small outcrop of rock and pointed to a small, hidden, cul-de-sac of beach filled with enormous rocks piled one on top of the other as if some giant had placed them there. Each rock was as large as his tent or five horses. Between them were narrow passageways of sand and shallow water.

"Come. I must show you."

She led him into a narrow crevice between two huge boulders. They squeezed through it single file, then crawled up a sloping rock that was slippery and hard to hang on to. Finally she led him out onto a flat surface of warm, grey stone, perched high above the sea.

"This is where I came to dream as a young girl."

She went to the edge and looked down at the waves splashing against the rocks, over at the horses nibbling on fresh grass, and far down the beach where the rest of the tribe had arrived and were setting up camp.

"They always go to the same place. It never changes. Come and sit with me."

She pulled the top of her tunic down and let it hang from her waist band, her upper body naked. Lying back on the warm stone, she put her hands behind her head and aimed her face up at the sun.

"When I was a young girl, I used to do this with no clothes but you are not ready for that," she said laughing.

He lay beside her, his bare chest feeling the warm sun but his eyes burning from the vision next to him. Though they had been together for days out in the desert, and she had been with Sabra and him many times, he hadn't realized how exquisite she was, as much or more so than his beloved Sabra.

"I am glad to see you smile once again," she said, the wind blowing her hair, long strands whipping across his chest. She noticed and tucked her hair under her head.

He closed his eyes and sighed.

"You will see," she whispered. "Time will cure the pain you feel."

"I don't think that is possible. How can I forget? I spent my entire life with Sabra. She was not only my half-sister but the woman closest to my heart, and now she is dead, killed by a mad woman who lays for eternity by her side. How can I ever forget?"

"You are a young, intelligent man who has a future. Alexandria will rise again and you will be there to make the library whole once more. This is something I know."

"Impossible. The library is gone. The scrolls are buried in a sealed tomb never to see the light of day again. The city is run by Romans, an evil priest, and a imbecile pharaoh."

"I tell you, Akhu. It will change."

"If it were only so."

Spray from a large wave rained down on them making them laugh.

"You see. You laugh. It will take time but you will be happy like the old days sooner than you know."

He sighed and closed his eyes.

A squawking gull woke him. Opening his eyes, he noticed she was gone and sat up. Her tunic was folded on the rock beside him. Quickly, he stood and looked all around. Fright took hold as another woman he had promised to keep safe had disappeared.

At the edge of the rock, he looked down and saw her swimming back toward the little beach. Though he was relieved, his heart jumped at the sight of her naked body swimming through the sea.

Though he tried to look away, his eyes would not obey and he watched Juji wade out of the water, disappear into the narrow crevice and then step out onto the flat surface where he stood.

She walked toward him, shaking her long hair, water flying in every direction, and stood naked in front of him.

"You look startled. I am sorry if I frightened you. I should have told you I was going for a swim."

"No. Yes... I mean it is all right. I just worried when I saw you were gone."

She picked up her toga and began to wrap it around her wet body then stopped.

"Would it be all right if I stayed this way? It is how I always was up here on my private rock."

"You may do whatever you wish," Akhu said in a halting voice.

"You may take off your loin cloth if you want," she said noticing his discomfort.

"I had better not. In fact, I should go see if the horses are all right.

He stood, embarrassed by the change her nakedness had created, and climbed down to the beach. The horses were fine so he wandered along the sand for a way then turned to go back to the rock.

She stood by the horses, her toga back on, her hands holding the reins of both animals.

"We had best join the others. There will be work to do."

The nomad village was up and operating by noon the following day. Everyone in the camp had an assigned task. It had been that way for ages and would be that way until time stood still.

"Your sister rides and works like a boy," Akhu said watching as Janis carried some drift wood for the evening fire.

"Little Janis has been that way ever since she was a child, always running, always out in front of everyone else, never satisfied with what she did and wanting more, always trying to be better.

"Sounds like her older sister," Akhu said smiling.

Juji, as one of the leaders, spent much of her time with the elders but, when she was free, worked beside Akhu who taught the young children.

Juji and Janis sat side by side as Akhu traced Greek letters in the sand. Each child did their best to make it look the same. Over and over, they practiced until he had them creating words, then short poems. The children were bright and eager, the elders thrilled at the learned man who came to them with their lost girl.

One day, while the children practiced, he asked Juji how she was taken by the slavers?

"I was but the age of Agra over there, maybe ten or so, I don't know. Two boys and I were at a well in an oasis getting the night water for the tribe. We heard a noise. I turned and a hood was thrown over my head and a hand over my mouth. Hours later, I was freed and found myself in the home of an old man and his sick wife. I took care of them. When he died, I was sold and taken to Alexandria to the home of a bad man, a merchant who had two other girl slaves. I learned the hard way and was often beaten if I did not do as told. When I refused to be his bed partner, I was caned badly and thrown out into the street. A good woman found me when she was out shopping and took me to her home and cured my wounds. One of her friends was Sabra who was looking for someone who could pass as her double. The consort wanted someone who looked like her twin."

"And that is how you met?"

"Yes, I gave her my life as a slave and as a friend."

"I know. You were always there, always, even when we...."

"Do not go to that place in your mind. It is over, Akhu."

He nodded and gave a deep sigh.

She found him sitting on the beach, staring out into the waves of a calm Mediterranean. Covered in sweat, he'd wandered off from the field of flax that the tribe was growing. She had seen him leave and wondered if she should go after him, There had been tears in his eyes and nothing worried her more.

An hour passed and she couldn't stand it. Setting her hoe down, Juji walked along the sand to where he sat and lowered herself beside him.

"Are you all right?"

He looked at her and nodded.

"It's just that every once in a while, her lack of being in my life overwhelms me."

"I understand. I too have been where distance separates me from those I love."

"You are very wise for your age but this is not space, it is time. It is forever."

Juji took his hand and held it as they stared out at some gulls diving for fish.

"Would you swim with me?"

"I don't know how."

"Come. I will show you."

She stood and removed her tunic, dropping it to the sand at her feet and stepped out of it, naked but for a necklace around her throat.

"Off. Take it off, Akhu."

He sighed and dropped his loincloth beside her tunic.

"Don't be so embarrassed. I have seen you like this many times with her."

"But, for some reason I feel traitorous doing this," he mumbled in embarrassment.

She took his hand and led him into the shallows. When they were waist high with small waves washing over them, she reached out and told him to lay his belly across her arms.

"Just lay out flat and kick your feet then sweep your arms back and forth."

"This is crazy," he said. "I'll never learn."

"Shh. Keep your mouth closed unless you want to drink the sea."

He paddled the water like a child, kicking fiercely and splashing water high in the air.

"You are doing well," she said her arms under his waist, still holding him on the surface.

Though he concentrated hard on doing as she asked, his mind was in a whirlwind of conflict. Her arm kept moving to keep a good grip as he swam, often going from his waist to the tops of his legs rubbing him midway and confusing him terribly. His thoughts went from swimming to feelings of arousal.

A big wave roared toward them. Seeing it, she rolled him toward her and wrapped her arms around him as the wave crashed in front of them. She crushed him to her bare breasts as the sea rolled overhead and drove them under water. As it thundered by she pushed up with her legs and they burst out into fresh, clean air. He coughed and spit out some of the sea he'd swallowed and looked into her wet face, hair streaming down over it, a huge smile creasing her mouth.

"That was wonderful," she said still holding him on the surface but tight against her breasts. "Now, I will let go. Swim to the beach."

She opened her arms and let him float away. He began thrashing with his legs and sweeping his arms. In only moments, his feet touched the sand and he stood, a big grin on his face.

"I swam. Did you see that. I actually swam."

But her mind was still back when she had held him, naked, and close against her body.

Evening came and the entire tribe sat around a fire, the women cooking, the men drinking the potent Egyptian beer that had made its way into the wilderness and her tribe.

She handed him a slightly burned piece of bread and refilled his cup.

"You don't need to wait on me. I can get it myself."

"But it is a pleasure and I want to," Juji said sitting beside him.

"Why are you so good to me?"

"It is what my friend, Sabra would wish."

He smiled and leaned back on his arms, a feeling of comfort and acceptance flooding him as he sipped his beer.

"So, this is the Egyptian," a man said coming up and standing over them with his muscular legs spread apart, his arms on his hips.

Juji jumped up and stood between them.

"It is you. I thought..."

"You wished, you mean. No. As you can see, I am quite well and as strong as ever."

She turned and spoke to Akhu who now stood beside her.

"This is Chamuchi, a man I once knew but who has been gone from the tribe."

"Once knew! Ha. This wench was mine. Had I not been made a slave she would be the mother of my children by now."

Akhu looked at her crimson face then back at Chamuchi with a frown.

"You make her uncomfortable with such talk," Akhu said stepping closer to the man.

"No Egyptian speaks to me like that nor will she embarrass me by sitting with a foreigner. Juji, you and Janis will come with me at once."

"I will not go with you again, never."

Akhu stepped up to the big man, his hand on the dagger in his loin cloth.

"You dare touch your dagger in my camp?" the man shouted

"Stand away from her," Akhu said in a calm voice.

Alarmed by the shouting a few other men came up.

"What is this about?" one asked.

"The foreigner takes my woman and insults me," Chamuchi said reaching for her arm.

Akhu's hand came down like a lightning bolt on his wrist, spinning the man to the left, then his other hand chopped down on his neck. Chamuchi fell to the sand on his hands and knees. For a moment, he kneeled there breathing hard then stood to face a furious Akhu.

"You will never touch her again. Never," Akhu threatened.

"Did you see what this Egyptian did?" Chamuchi said to the others. "I will have my satisfaction."

With that he stormed off into the night.

"What was that all about," Akhu said after everyone had left and they were alone again.

"He is not a good man and has never been. Yet, what he says is true. I was fifteen. He came to me in the fields, dragged me into the bushes over there," she said pointing, "and took my girlhood from me."

"I'm so sorry, Juji. I didn't know."

"He will ask the elders for a fight to the death. They will allow it even though I will speak in your defense."

"He is a big man but..."

"Be careful, Akhu. He is not to be trusted to fight fairly."

The following night, Akhu, dressed in a tight loin cloth was led by Juji to the center of the village where a circle had been scratched in the sand, an oval about three strides in diameter.

"You must stay within that circle," she said as they stood waiting for Chamuchi to arrive.

Many of the tribe were there, nervously standing in small groups, knowing what was about to happen.

"Leave your dagger with me. It must be done with your bare hands."

Akhu was a strong as any man but a head shorter than Chamuchi who arrived among a group of his friends, his head shaved, his naked body smeared with chicken fat.

Juji handed him a gourd filled with oil and reached down to remove his loin cloth.

"Help me rub this oil onto your skin," she said to little Janis who stood by her side, eyes angry yet quiet as usual." It will make it harder for him to grasp you."

She dipped her fingers into the oil and smoothed it on his shoulders while Janis did the same to his chest.

Chamuchi stepped into the ring and hunched over, his feet wide apart, his long arms hanging down, an expression on his face that made Juji's heart pound with fear.

Akhu walked into the ring and stood looking at the ferocious sight in front of him, sizing up his opponent, looking for a weak spot, and finding none.

Chamuchi moved forward, one foot in front of the other, his hands still hanging by his sides as he came toward Akhu in a low crouch.

Akhu stood firmly on two legs planted deep in the sand and waited. Chamuchi's hand shot out and thudded into Akhu's chest, a blow he felt all the way to his knees. Then, the other hand shot forward which Akhu grabbed with his two hands and pulled toward him with all his strength. Akhu, still holding his slippery arm, turned and ducked. Chamuchi flew over his shoulder and landed on his back in the sand behind him.

Akhu turned as Chamuchi gathered himself and stood to face him again. Blood ran from a cut on his cheek, his eyes flaming in anger.

He rushed Akhu, his immense body hitting him in the midsection and knocking Akhu down with Chamuchi on top of him, his hands around his throat. Akhu struggled, clawing at the hands choking him, but could not get a solid grip on them, his fingers slipping on the chicken fat.

Juji screamed as Chamuchi bit Akhu's arm, digging his teeth deep into Akhu's flesh, blood spurting onto his face.

In great pain and realizing his life was almost over, Akhu reached out with his other arm, grabbed a handful of sand and threw it into the bloody face of Chamuchi. The man screamed as Akhu quickly squirmed loose from his grip and rolled over in the sand, his foot on the edge of the circle. He staggered to his feet to see Chamuchi standing in front of him, bloodshot eyes, glaring at him in hatred.

"You will die," Chamuchi shouted and rushed Akhu who stepped aside. The man turned and rushed again, grabbing Akhu's arm which slipped from his fingers.

Akhu, clasped both of his hands together in a fist and raised them like a club over his head. When Chamuchi rushed him again, he brought his fists down on his head just an instant before the running body slammed into his chest. All went black and Akhu fell to the sand not knowing if Isis had taken him to the land of the gods or not.

A warm hand slipped behind his head as he opened his eyes. Juji kneeled beside him, her beautiful olive colored body over him, and a smile on her face. Janis stood behind her, her face smeared with the fighting oil, silent but relieved.

"You have won, Akhu. Your blow to the head killed him but it was not enough to stop his charge into you. I am free of his threats thanks to you. If you can stand, I will take you to the sea and clean your body of his filthy hands."

Akhu staggered to his feet and looked down at Chamuchi, his head twisted in an odd direction, the life gone from dull eyes staring up at him.

She took his oily hand and led him to the edge of the sea where he sat in the sand, small waves washing over his legs as she bathed him, wiping away the oil and blood and sand, slowly cleaning and caressing his hurts with her soft, warm hands

"You did a very brave thing in the ring," she said. "No man has ever fought for me before. I thank you from the bottom of my heart."

Akhu smiled then winced as she wiped sand from a cut on his hip.

"Do you know that I have been happy here." Akhu said watching her hands move slowly along his thigh. "That is until today when this happened?"

"Yes, I have seen joy in your eyes. It is good that you are forgetting and moving on with life."

"I will never forget her but you have been good medicine for me. No one else would have cared."

"I loved her too. She saved my life and taught me much. She also brought you to me for which I thank the gods."

"Juji, that is not to be. I cannot..."

"Shh. lean back there is another cut here on your waist."

The flax was harvested and the summer came to a close. The elders sat and discussed the coming move into the desert before the rains came along with mosquitoes and disease that the wet weather brought.

Akhu had gained full recognition as a member of the tribe and was looked on with respect. His teaching of the children bore fruit as ten boys and Janis had learned Greek to the point where they sat at the night fires and recited to the gathered tribe.

"It is like the Greeks who have done this for centuries," Akhu said smiling. "Just listen to her. She speaks like a learned Greek."

"Young Janis will grow to be a leader because of you, a smart woman, a teacher, who will bring great things to the tribe."

He smiled again looking into the bright eyes of Juji who sat beside him, bare to the waist as were all the women, short skirt barely covering, and long brown legs, tanned by the sun from long hours they spent on the flat rock overlooking the sea. Juji had become his best friend, a friendship rivaling that of One Eye or even Sabra, something he wondered about. No one had ever been as loyal or trustworthy. And Juji was even approaching Sabra's wealth of knowledge.

Juji and Janis had some months ago begun attending his school sessions with the children and soaked up knowledge as fast as he could recite. Juji's interest in world history amazed him and he wished out loud that they had access to the scrolls of Alexandria library.

"You have told me they are sealed in the tomb," she said.

"Forever. The slave told us the pharaoh, the queen, and my sister have been sealed with rocks and mortar, sealed in a hidden chamber out of the reach of robbers and thieves."

"But you are the one who designed the tomb. Is that not right?"

"Yes. I designed it but I wasn't there to see if any changes were made, if it is the same as I drew on rolls and rolls of papyrus."

"The entombment was rushed as the Romans approached the city. What changes could be made in such a short time. They were probably busy trying to complete the burials in a great hurry."

"If that is true the scrolls remain deep in the tomb, in a secret chamber only a few know about."

"It is a shame that they will never see the light of day. Think of the knowledge buried there?"

"I know, Juji. I know."

Before the tribe broke camp for the desert, they held what was called, The Games, an event performed near the sea for as long as anyone could remember. All men over the age of nine participated and became a member of a team.

It began at dawn, the first runner of each team standing on a line drawn in the sand. The route each man would take led up the beach into the sea around the rocky outcrop, past the pile of boulders Akhu and Juji used as their hide-away, for a considerable distance beyond, then a turn at a dead end and a sprint back to the starting point where the next man waited anxiously for his lap.

Akhu's team had one young boy, two of the elders, and a couple of men he didn't know. The young boy, a youth of ten, was as slim and fast as any of the men. He led off and came back second. But the two elders, out of shape from too much beer and bread, failed to keep his lead. The next two on his team held their own until it was Akhu's turn. When his teammate raced to the line, touching Akhu's hand as he dashed by, Akhu sprinted away, neck and neck with two others.

He ran as fast as his legs would go, splashed around the big, rocky outcrop and across the familiar sand in front of the mounds of boulders. Making a quick decision, he decided to squeeze through the narrow crevice that only he and Juji knew about, in the hope of bursting out the other side and avoiding the long run through the water around the enormous mountain of stone.

He ran directly at the huge rocks while the other two laughed and plunged into the water to make their way around the tumbled mass of boulders.

Akhu, out of breath, squeezed and slid along the narrow ravine with sea water up to his knees, his hands reaching for a grip to help pull him along. Then, clawing his way up and over a fallen rock, he burst out into the sun a good five paces ahead of the other two racers.

All the way to the finish line, he heard the yells of encouragement, the loudest coming from Juji, then total exhaustion when he crossed and fell to the ground gasping for breath.

"You did it. You won for our team," she shouted leaning over and giving him a kiss on the cheek.

Though exhausted, his heart jumped at her kiss. He looked, dazed and half out of it, into the smiling face Sabra but quickly saw it was Juji. Yet, the bright, happy eyes looking down at him made his heart pounded in the same way.

Chapter Twenty Two - The False Queen

The trek into the desert and the winter oasis lasted two days. Finally, camp was set up and life resumed its normal pace.

They sat by the evening fire, side by side, sipping from the same cup and sharing a piece of bread.

"I had a strange dream last night," she said. "Sabra sat on the throne but the view I had was from her eyes."

Akhu looked at her, a serious expression on his face. "The gods make our dreams. What could it mean?"

"In the dream, I looked down at my hands, Sabra's hands, and saw the pharaoh's scepter in her hands, my hands. I woke in a cold sweat."

He didn't say a word for five minutes then looked at her and said, "Come with me. We must talk privately."

She took his hand as they walked out into the desert and sat on a rock. A million stars blinked overhead.

"Your dream may be a prophesy."

"What do you mean?"

"That you are to be the pharaoh."

"Do not toy with me, Akhu. I am a simple nomad girl not used to such joking."

"Think for a moment. Just hear me out," he said sitting up straighter and taking her hand in his. "I don't know why I haven't thought of this before. You look more like Sabra than she does herself. You know her better than anyone including me who knew her from childhood. You watched and listened to everything that was said and done around her. You loved her as I do."

"But..."

He reached into the top of his tunic and pulled out the scroll signed and marked in wax by the dead pharaoh, the one making Sabra regent before the eighth birthday of his son, the heir.

"This makes Sabra the Pharaoh regent of Egypt, "he said almost breathless. "What if you became Sabra??

"You make fun of me. I could never do that."

"There are times when I feel I am with her when I am next to you. Why would other people doubt?"

For a moment, he saw how what he had said upset her.

"I mean that, whey would other people ever question it?"

"Because I am not her."

"I can teach you. I will make you Sabra and you will take the rule of Egypt away from that man who is not well in the head and the evil high priest who rules in his name."

"You are serious."

"I am. We will think and plan. We will say the woman stabbed by the queen was Juji, the slave who was used often as her double. Many knew this, at least enough to make it bear witness. We will say the pharaoh is entombed with an imposter at his side, the woman called Juji, and that you are the Sabra that the pharaoh decreed Regent and the one he wanted to rule Egypt. The high priest cannot contest this order of his pharaoh."

He held the scroll out for her to see.

Juji sat by his side, her head in her hands, breathing heavily and wondering if all he said was possible or just some crazy dream to bring his beloved Sabra back to the world of the living?

"We would no longer have this," she said looking up at the blinking stars overhead.

The next few weeks were a nightmare for Juji as Akhu talked of nothing else, his plan developing as the days progressed. He spent hours telling her of the things they had done as children before she was taken by the slavers. But, though he tried to remember everything, there were gaps in the years she spent as a captive, facts that had to be as accurate as possible in the unlikely event someone who had known her during those bad times would show up.

"But a queen can deny anything, can she not?" Juji asked.

"Of course. I have heard pharaoh say things that were not true," he said. "No one dared challenge him."

"Then, you should not worry."

But, she was the one who worried. Could she really pull this off? Akhu was so determined, so sure that it was possible. But what if she made a mistake? And maybe what really worried her was the way Akhu loved his Sabra? Every story he told of their growing up was one of the deep fondness of two people who were as entwined as two mating snakes.

She bit her lip and said, "When Akhu? When do we do this thing?"

"The anniversary of the Pharaoh's death is in one month. We should arrive then?"

"One month and I will no longer be Juji?"

"That is so."

"Will you miss Juji?" she asked.

"I will always be with you, to help and guide you when you need me."

"But that will be with Sabra. I asked if you will miss Juji?"

"You begin to sound like a queen. Yes, I will miss the girl I have become so fond of but you will be there as my sister, the Regent pharaoh."

"You have grown fond of me as Juji?"

"Yes. It has been a difficult time but I have grown very close to you as my friend."

"It is important to me that you feel this way. Please never forget it or these times we have had together. I, for one, will never forget a moment of them."

Akhu nodded that he understood but failed to notice the tears in her eyes.

Over and over they rehearsed the role Juji was to play. As she had dressed Sabra and done her hair and makeup, there was no need to practice that. So, Akhu kept going back to the time of Sabra's slavery looking for problems or gaps they could not fill in.

"What do we say to the tribe?" she asked one afternoon when the date for departure was close.

Akhu thought for a minute, a question he had not considered.

"Could we say that Akhu yearns for his home, wishes to return and wants me to go with him?" she asked.

"But what if someone who knows you well comes to Alexandria and sees you as queen?"

"I will convince him as I do the others that I am Sabra not Juji. We will insist that Juji died."

Akhu nodded his head that he agreed. There were so many possibilities of trouble.

"And what do we say when I step into the palace grounds? she asked in that new voice that had begun to sound regal and authoritative.

"I have thought long and hard on this," he said. "I believe we should just appear and see the effect it has on the high priest."

She shook her head.

"No. I think we should arrive as a queen who has been gone for a year, a queen who expects her crown to be handed over to her when she steps forward. I wish to enter the city in a fine chariot with armed horsemen as my guard."

"But where will we get it and the horsemen?"

She smiled.

"A queen can command what she wishes. We will go to Aswan and get what I require."

It was a sad day when Juji left her tribe. The elders accepted her excuse that Akhu wished to return to his city and help in the rebuilding of Alexandria. Janis cried but smiled when Juji said she could come to Alexandria when the tribe moved to the summer place at the sea.

They rode off on a camel for the distant city of Aswan, Juji with tears in her eyes as she looked back at her waving sister and the home she had known and loved.

Aswan, on the River Nile, was a bustling, commercial city. With coins of gold, they purchased six horses and six men who had once been trained soldiers. Juji bought the most expensive thin linen that could be found and had it made into a full length gown that hung from small straps on her shoulders, as light as air that draped softly over her magnificent body, and touched the ground. It felt strange after such a long time of having been bare to the waist like the rest of her tribe but she knew it must be so. She, however, insisted the seamstress make the front open as far as her waist.

Akhu had a tunic made of equally fine cotton and, at Juji's insistence, had the seamstress shorten it to the Roman length of half way up his thigh.

A boat was hired, a boat large enough to carry six horses, a chariot and its two white mares, plus a tent that shaded the elegant woman who sat on a chair, the cool river breeze tugging at her long hair that had been teased into the style of a queen.

Five days later, the boat docked along the quay in Alexandria. Akhu was noticeably nervous as he looked into his beloved city, half rebuilt, half still in ruins.

But he also noticed a soldier, who had been standing nearby as the boat docked. the man looked carefully, then walked rapidly toward the palace.

"We have been seen already," Akhu whispered.

An hour was spent preparing the procession. Juji, dressed in her fine new gown, sat in the chariot with Akhu holding the reins of the white mares. Three of the six mounted guards rode ahead and three behind, all dressed with armor and carrying long swords belted at the hip.

Akhu slapped the reins on the mare's backs and they trotted off toward the palace.

Juji pressed her thigh against his leg seeking some comfort from the nervousness she felt. It was one thing practicing to be a queen but quite another to be one.

As they neared the palace, she said, "You will no longer address me as Juji. I am Sabra from this moment on."

He drew a deep breath and nodded that he understood though in his heart he knew she could be no one but Juji.

The palace gates opened and allowed the chariot and its mounted guards to enter. The captain of the palace guard stepped up to Akhu and asked what their business was.

"Queen Sabra wishes an audience with the high priest. Tell him Akhu brings her to reclaim her throne."

The man looked at her, then back at Akhu, a man he thought he recognized and almost choked saying, "But, she is...."

Juji glared down at him as Akhu picked up the reins expecting his order to be obeyed.

The captain turned and barked an order to a soldier who had come out to see what was going on. The man ran off toward the palace.

"Do I recognize you, sir?" the captain said.

"I am Akhu, once the librarian of the Mouseion which I see is now in ruins."

"Yes. yes. I once served you when the tomb was being built. Welcome home."

"Thank you, captain. May we proceed?"

"I will have my men escort you."

He called into the small building. Five soldiers ran out and sprinted in front of the chariot as they made their way into the palace grounds and stopped in front of the stone steps that led up to the luxurious quarters of the pharaoh.

On the top step, the high priest stood glaring down a them, older and fatter, but just as vicious looking as ever.

"You return, master Akhu. All thought you dead along with the others."

Akhu said nothing just dismounted from the chariot and offered his hand to Juji. She took it and stepped with one elegantly sandaled foot onto the rail and planted her feet on the soil of the land she hoped to rule.

He led her up the steps, her guard following close behind. Five Roman soldiers stood in the shadows out of sight.

Akhu, a fierce and serious expression on his face, stepped in front of the high priest.

"Queen Sabra returns and will assume her throne."

The priest looked at Juji, his eyes narrowed and full of questions.

"I myself placed the light heart of the woman you speak of, placed it in her hollowed out chest and sealed it with aromatic linens. I spoke over her dead body as the coffin was sealed with lead. Are you telling me this woman has been brought back from the dead?"

"She did not die. It was her double, the slave Juji who died. Queen Sabra escaped at my hand and has returned to claim the throne from the usurper and his advisor."

The high priest flushed red and coughed. The Roman soldiers moved restlessly but stayed where they were.

"You come with five or six armed men and have the audacity to think you can take over the crown with mere words. It would take an army to do what you propose."

"We need no army," Akhu said. "All we need are just men who will listen and act."

"Ha! Why do I spend my precious time out in the sun listening to the words of a maniac?"

"Because he speaks for me," Juji said in a firm, soft voice. "You will call an assembly of the priests and governors at once."

The priest looked at her and smiled.

"I will gladly do so. They deserve a good laugh at an imposters expense. But, your head will leave that lovely but traitorous body when the assembly is done with you."

He turned and stormed into the palace. A slave ran forward and led them to a waiting room then closed the door behind him.

"Are you ready for what is to come?' Akhu asked sitting in a chair.

She paced the room, back and forth, then turned to him and smiled.

"If it goes well I will be queen and you will be rewarded. If not, you will be at my side as our heads roll into the sand. Either way, we are in this together."

A knock sounded on the door and a well dressed man entered.

"I am Consul Pretorious, assigned by Rome as the governor of this city. You will come and sit beside me to face the Pharaoh and the priest. He tells me you have made bold claims which we will hear."

With that, he motioned for them to follow. They went out of the room, down a long hallway, and into the throne room where the dead king Nebrunef's mentally retarded brother sat in the pharaoh chair, a blank expression on his face, a bib around his neck wet with drool.

The high priest stood in front of the pharaoh in his hooded robes of death, black linen that covered all but his hands and pale face.

Standing on the sides of the room were many Akhu recognized, men who he had worked with on the tomb and at the library, men he considered fair and just. But, there were also many Romans, some were soldiers but others looked like businessmen come to trade with rich Egypt.

She walked in front of him, as regal as any queen, her gown flowing loosely over the incredible body so many in the room knew by sight. She stopped, stood tall, chin up, eyes forward, only a few paces before the priest and pharaoh. Akhu came up and stood by her side.

"This, my king, is the imposter who claims your throne."

The slack expression on the pharaoh's face did not change.

"I myself embalmed and buried your brother, King Nebrunef, your mother, Queen Paqui, and Sabra the second consort," he said, still looking at and addressing the pharaoh. "I gave them the finest burial Egypt has ever seen and supervised the placing of the stones to seal their journey to the afterlife forever."

The king, unable to truly understand what was going on, leaned forward and squinted his eyes. The priest turned to face the crowd.

"If it were not so laughable, I would have killed them at the gate for making such an audacious claim against our king. But, I have brought them here for your enjoyment before they are dispatched for Osiris's punishment."

A murmur went through those assembled along the sides of the hall.

"Am I not allowed to speak," Juji said looking at the pharaoh who gave her a crooked smile and stared at the open front of her gown.

He grinned and nodded his approval.

She addressed him and no one else.

"Do you not remember my holding you when your mother and father were gone?"

He looked at the priest then back at her and nodded.

"Do you not remember my holding your hand when that storm, filled with thunder and lightning, shook the palace?"

He smiled and nodded vigorously.

"What does this have to do with your ridiculous claim?" the priest laughed.

"He recognizes his friend, Sabra."

"Even if that were so," the priest said halting for a moment realizing he'd made a mistake, "What does that have to do with anything?"

She turned to face the crowd.

"It verifies that you look at Sabra, the rightful Regent named by your dead Pharaoh, King Nebrunef."

The crowd mumbled. A few Roman soldiers put their hands on the hilt of their short swords.

"I laugh," the priest said.

"You laugh at your king's last order, one you saw him sign and seal," she said holding up the scroll

Akhu had carried through rain and battle and guarded with his life.

"Let me see that," the priest said reaching forward.

She turned away from the priest and held it out in front of her.

"I call on the priests of Horus and Isis to read it aloud."

The two men stepped forward and took the scroll from her hands, both visibly nervous as the high priest glared at them.

They broke the seal and read aloud from the scroll, words that echoed off the walls of an absolutely silent room, words that ordered Sabra to be Regent for eight years until her son, Thet, his heir would become pharaoh.

"The boy heir died at the hands of traitors but I live and stand before you as your queen. I will make sure my friend, the present king, is well cared for and lives a happy life. But, I will be your new pharaoh and rule as a wise and good queen."

The murmurs became a mumble then the room filled with voices.

"Quiet," she said in a low but authoritative tone.

The room went silent. She turned to the pharaoh who was wiping his wet chin.

"I will make you my counselor of joy and laughter. We will have some of those good times we once had. No more will you be made a joke of by this man."

She turned to the high priest.

"Drop to your knees and pledge your allegiance to Sabra, Pharaoh of Egypt or I will have your head."

The priest looked around at the stunned faces of everyone in the room, his eyes wide in disbelief, but wise enough to realize he must do what she demanded or die, his mind racing and convincing him his day of reckoning would come.

"I yield to my queen," he said falling to his knees. "But, I have many questions?"

"You will speak when I give permission," she said then turned to the pharaoh and took his hand. "I have many stories to tell you of the wonders outside these palace walls."

"Take the priest to his quarters and secure him in his rooms until he is summoned," Akhu said to the soldiers then turned to her,. "My queen, we must meet with the governors at once."

She smiled at the ex-pharaoh whose hand she held, and said, "You see, already they wish me to govern and not play with my friend. I will come to you later as promised."

She sat on the throne, nervous but using all her powers to keep it from showing. Akhu stood by her side.

The door to the consul chambers opened and eleven men, led by the high priest, entered the room to bow and stand in front of her.

She smiled at them.

"It is good to see you again, Governor Thadeus, and you, Gemma. And look at good Acta, how you have grown.. It is a great pleasure to see all of you survived the great fire."

Then nodded that they too were happy to have survived.

"I have called this meeting for two purposes," she said folding the opening to her gown closed as it was distracting the men. "First is to reaffirm your positions in my government. You will notice that some are missing. You will present candidates to replace them."

She looked directly at the priest and went on, "The Romans are not attending this meeting on purpose. I wish to know who is cooperating with them, what the costs to my treasury are for peace, and who leads them?"

Governor Thadeus stepped forward and bowed his head.

"The people, realizing all was lost, have done their best to accommodate the invaders. The Romans have placed a single Prefect as the head of their forces, a good man but who ages rapidly under the task."

"I met him. He seems like a fair man." Akhu said.

"And who leads them?"

"That is difficult to say," the high priest offered.

"If you know, why is it difficult to tell your queen?"

He reddened down to his thin neck.

"At the time of the attack, four legions came through the walls with our meager five thousand soldiers to defend our city," he said. "They fought bravely but were overwhelmed. Only one legion remains, the Eighth led by a General Ponticus."

"And is he the Roman's leader?"

"Yes, I believe so," the priest said withering under her hard stare.

"You believe so? I need men around me who are sure of what they say. Advise me by noon tomorrow if what you say is true."

He nodded and left the room backing away as was custom.

"Now, I wish to make my intentions clear about the coronation ceremony. It will not be a public spectacle but one done in private, in the throne room with one hundred commoners representing the people plus the palace officials. Expense will be kept to the minimum. We have a city to rebuild not to honor a new pharaoh."

The men had shocked expressions on their faces but nodded in agreement.

"We will have the coronation tomorrow. Also invite the prefect and this General Ponticus. I want them to hear what I have to say."

Her advisers nodded and backed out of the room.

"My god, Ju..., my queen," Akhu whispered, "What has gotten into you."

"You said act like a pharaoh. I have done just that."

He smiled and took her hand to help her off the throne, not failing to feel the dampness of her palm.

Juji was being dressed by her maids while the ex-pharaoh sat on the floor playing with dice she found amused him, a game she'd enjoyed in her youth. She stood naked in front of a polished bronze reflecting disk as a maid piled her dark hair high on her head in the honeycombed style of royalty and placed a gold pin the size of her palm to hold it in place. Two gold straight pins pierced the nest of hair, two pins shaped like twisting serpents.

A pair of maids bathed her body in scented water, patted her dry, then rubbed aromatic oils all over so she glistened like sunlight on still water. Her feet were bound in papyrus sandals laced with gold, straps winding up her bare legs to her knees.

Another pair of maids entered the room carrying a gown across their outstretched arms, a sheet of cloth of the sheerest, white linen, so light it had almost no weight at all. Juji held out her arms as the girls lowered it over her head, a square hole in the cloth fell onto her shoulders, the remainder tumbling to the floor.

She smiled and turned to see the back. A flap of linen hung straight down in front, another in back, her glistening bare skin showing all the way up the sides.

"This should show the conservative ones how I wish to free Egypt," she said as one of the maids tied a sash around the middle. "I should go without the sash but I don't want to move too fast."

Her maids, all bare to the waist as was custom in her nomad village, smiled, already enjoying the freedom she promised.

She was handed a single white Lilly which she clasped in her hand and walked to the door. A maid opened it and she moved like a gracious queen into the throne room.

The mumble of voices hushed as she entered and walked to the throne. Ascending the steps, she turned and sat with her bare arms on the carved lions, the flaps of her gown hiding little of her body.

The young priest of Horus came forward and spoke in ancient Egyptian, a dialect no one but the priests understood. The high priest glared at him and then at her, angry at having been denied his rightful job.

In the back of the room, she saw the Prefect and a man who must have been General Ponticus standing beside Akhu. Beside them was her sister, Janis, newly arrived at court, looking grown up in a long, linen dress. She had never seen her in anything but a loin cloth before. .

Two young priests came to her with the symbols of power in their hands. One spoke slowly and quietly as he placed the scepter, a long, gold staff, in her hand. The other placed a golden orb in her lap, a round ball of solid gold the size of a melon and carved with many symbols dating back a thousand years. For a moment he hesitated then gave her the Ankh oval and cross, the sacred symbol of fertility since the beginning of time.

He turned for the crown of gold.

"Please, priest. May I have another put it on my head?"

"Of course, my queen."

"Master Akhu, please come forward."

Akhu looked at the two Romans, shrugged his shoulders, and walked to the throne, bowed and stood before her.

"This man has saved your queen's life so many times during our flight that I cannot count them. I owe all of this to him. Henceforth, Master Akhu will lead the task of rebuilding the Mouseion and become my chief advisor."

A small murmur rose from the officials of the kingdom but quieted when she went on.

"Place the crown, Master Akhu."

He stepped forward, took the gold crown from the hands of the young priest, and approached. Her beautiful face, shining with happiness, looked up at him, her eyes watering with tears as the magnitude of what they were doing finally sank in.

He gave her a secret wink and raised the crown over her head, lowered it and placed it among the dark locks of hair that smelled of almonds.

The room exploded in cheers and hand claps, all but the high priest who stood and stared with an expression of pure hatred.

Chapter Twenty Three - Consummation

A maid came for him at midnight and led him to the queen's chambers.

"He is here," the maid said to the darkened room and closed the door behind her.

"I am here by the window," Juji's voice said from the darkness.

He walked to where the sound came from and stood beside her. She took his hand in hers.

"Those wonderful days by the sea on our secret rock are gone forever, are they not?"

"Yes, my queen. They are gone forever."

"But we remember, don't we?"

"I have never been as happy as I was in your village."

"I stand here and think the same thing and wonder if we should not give up this charade and go back to where we were at peace? I can feel the intrigue and scheming in the air? It is everywhere, the high priest, the Romans, those we don't even know. I fear we have taken on more than we can chew."

"I have been nothing but amazed at how just and fair all your commands have been. You, as I predicted, will be the best pharaoh Egypt has ever known."

"I need you by my side, Akhu. Please do not desert me."

"I will die at your side, my queen."

"I command you not to die and hope you are only playing with me to say such a thing/"

He smiled and said, "I am your most loyal subject, Queen Sabra."

She shook her head.

"When we are alone, can I not be who I am?"

"Never again."

She sighed and looked up at him from the darkness.

"Do you approve?"

"Approve what?"

"I have told my maids and those of my household they may dress as the Egyptians did four dynasties ago and as we dressed in my village. Women may go about bare on the top if they wish. Men may wear but brief loin clothes or roman skirts. Not just the servants and slaves but anyone who wishes. I yearn for as much freedom as this land can take."

He looked at her standing by the open window in the dark, naked but for a narrow cloth around her waist.

"I approve whatever you think is good for Egypt."

"Then you will also approve of my freeing the household slaves. I wish those around me to be free to speak their minds if they have something of value to say."

"It will be a problem but can be done. Most of the slaves are on our ships and those who work in our mines are captured soldiers. But, as I think about it, you are wise to free those around you who can be of help if they are not bound by a slaves silence."

"And what do you plan for the new Mouseion?"

"To tell you the truth, I haven't had time to think much about it?"

"The reason I have brought you this night, so late and so secretly, is that I also have thought about the Mouseion. I wish your library to be great again but it cannot be without the vast knowledge it once held."

"But that is buried in the tomb along with ...."

"That is the problem. How do we free the scrolls?"

Akhu looked at her face, now as serious as he had ever seen it, a face that glistened in the moon light, eyes alert and flashing with excitement.

"I fear there is nothing that can be done," he said sadly. "The tomb has been sealed with huge stones mortared in place. It would be a sacrilege to open the tomb and the priests would never allow it.

If we tried and were discovered, you could lose your throne and your head."

She smiled and looked out the window and into the courtyard below.

"But thieves rob the tombs all the time. How do they do it? How do they get away with it?"

"They are outlaws and when caught are beheaded for their crimes. There are some in your dungeon right now, thieves who were not caught robbing a tomb but who were turned in by a spy who heard them planning such a thing."

"Perhaps one should question them as to what they had planned before caught?"

"Are you suggesting that I...."

"The more knowledge a queen has the better she can govern."

She stood, her body brushing by his, and went to her rooms leaving Akhu standing by the window wondering if what he had heard was what he thought she had said.

Juji was now Queen Sabra. Her orders were his to do without question. He took a deep breath and left her chambers, nodding to the maid as she closed the door behind him.

Chapter Twenty Four - Dorian, the Gypsy

The smell was almost unbearable as he stepped carefully on slippery, stone steps leading to the dungeon below. A pair of guards had actually patted his toga to be sure he carried nothing into the dungeon, then they had opened a thick, wood door and pointed the way down.

A few torches burned in wall sconces giving just enough light to see. At the bottom of the stairs, he looked at six empty cells, a seventh at the far end, however, held ten men. He approached as they stood and came to the iron bars.

A big man with wild red hair stepped forward, his hands defiantly on his hips.

"A noble comes to visit, my friends." he said laughing.

Akhu stepped as close to the bars as was safe and stood looking into the eyes of the enormous man, a soiled loin cloth wrapped loosely around his waist, sweat and dirt covering his muscular body.

"You are the tomb robber I am told," Akhu said staring him in the eyes.

"I am a simple gypsy found guilty of a crime that had not been committed."

"I have lived with the gypsies and know they will only tell the truth to one who is of their blood."

The man laughed.

"You lived with gypsies? Ha. Do you hear that men? He claims to have been a gypsy before he became a rich and powerful noble man."

Some of them laughed.

"I have ridden their camels into the far desert, drunk their terrible wine, fought in the ring of death and survived. I know a thing or two about you and your men."

The leer on the big man left his face and he came closer.

"Who are you?"

"I am called Akhu. I honor the nomad code of justice and will see you are released after you pay the debt you will owe me."

"Released to be killed?"

"No, my friend, released to return to your land more wealthy than you can imagine."

The others came closer as Akhu's voice became quieter and more conspiratorial.

"What is it you wish us to do for such a thing?"

"I want you to rob a tomb."

The others looked back and forth at each other as a smile crossed their leader's face.

"You will allow us to rob a tomb and then release us? What is this, some kind of joke?"

"A very serious proposition which you are in no position to refuse."

"When would we do this thing?"

"Tomorrow night. I will have horses and carts waiting at the far gates. A maid will come and lead you to where they will be."

"The guards?"

"They will be taken care of. Do not worry about them."

"You will lead us to this tomb?"

"I will and I then show you how to enter without anyone ever knowing you have been there."

The men looked at each other, nodding and mumbling among themselves.

"Do I have your word?" Akhu asked.

"You have the word of Dorian, the gypsy."

"I leave now. Follow the maid that comes for you."

He turned and made his way up the dark, slippery steps to the light of day.

At the queen's orders, the reconstruction of the Mouseion was well underway, its vast number of buildings of stone only needing superficial repairs to bring them back to life. Furnishings were brought and library shelves were constructed by slave carpenters, empty shelves to hold non-existent scrolls.

Akhu slept until dusk, rose, put on his work tunic, strapped his long sword to his waist, and stepped out into the late afternoon sun.

The guards at the dungeon had been given rotten food laced with a slight amount of a sleeping potion. When they awoke, they would be punished for sleeping while their prisoners escaped but forgiven by the Queen as unable to stop them because of the awful sickness that plagued their bellies. It would be decided that they had eaten bad food which caused them to retch and pass out from pain.

Akhu's horse took him into the desert and the Valley of the Dead where King Nebrunef's tomb sat among other tombs in the darkness. The maid waited with the men as he galloped up to them.

Each of the ten men sat astride a horse attached by leather ropes to a cart. Akhu approached and rode up to the big man, Dorian, and his ferocious looking red beard.

"Follow me," he said as the column of men, horses, and carts wheeled off toward a stone structure as high as the palace itself.

Akhu led them away from the sealed entrance, around to the north side and stopped in front of a wall of solid stones all perfectly mortared in place.

"Dig here," he said pointing at the foot of a particular flat, faced stone.

Four men dismounted and began digging at the base of the stone. Six feet down they scraped onto something solid which they quickly uncovered.

"Remove it," Akhu said.

All the men jumped into the hole and dug their fingers around an immense stone, leaned back and heaved until it moved a few inches. They heaved some more, puffing and shouting in Gypsy until it was tipped upright.

A dark hole appeared below what the stone had covered.

"We go down there," Akhu said sliding down and onto the narrow landing then putting a foot on a carved stone step.

Down he went followed by the men. The steps narrowed and turned to the right then went straight toward the center of the tomb.

"This is not the entombment chambers," Dorian said, his voice sounding hollow and muffled in the passage.

"No, we go to the room of treasures."

The big man smiled and followed him, Akhu's torch leading the way.

At his instructions, another flat stone, that looked much like all the others, was moved aside and they entered a dark room.

"Here," Akhu said. "Be very careful how you handle them. Gently take each one to the carts outside and cover them with those wraps I have given you."

"But there are no treasures here. These are nothing but scrolls of the dead," Dorian shouted.

"You will not take anything but these scrolls. There are many so let us begin. You will be richly rewarded when they are safely in the new library."

Dorian, sensing he had no other choice, nodded and told his men to handle them carefully and to proceed quickly.

For the rest of the night, the men made many trips from the treasure room back to their carts.

Finally, as light threatened in the east, the column of horses and carts made their way toward the city.

"We have left the tomb as it was a day ago," Akhu said as they rode. "Your men did an excellent job of concealing our entry way. But, I must tell you. It is not the way to the entombments should you ever wish to return. The Pharaoh and his attendants entrance is far more difficult to find."

"If your promise of reward is good, we will never have a need to return."

Akhu smiled at this corrupt gypsy knowing full well it was an empty promise.

The carts made their way through deserted streets, into the Mouseion complex, and to the library just as dawn peeked over the hills. They worked unseen inside the courtyard of the library, taking the scrolls and placing them on the new built shelves. By afternoon, 550,,000 of the original 700,000 were back where they belonged.

Akhu looked at the tired men and smiled.

"You have done well, my friends. A commercial chariot waits outside, one big enough for ten men and a wooden cask filled with what Gypsies love best."

They shook hands as one of the gypsy men came running in.

"We must leave before the vultures see what is in the chariot. You will not believe the gold that sits in a simple wood box."

Dorian clasped Akhu's hand in the Roman style, then kissed his cheek as the gypsies do.

"Farewell, Akhu. If you are ever in need come to us. A brother is always welcome."

"I will do that, Dorian. Thank you."

The men raced off to see what was in the chariot then left as quickly as the horses could run.

"I have heard the library is complete and many of the missing scrolls sit on the shelves," Juji said as they walked along a path in the courtyard.

"Yes, it is a miracle. It is said they were found in a secret storage place untouched by the fires."

"I am pleased the library is once again ready to offer all who come for access to the world's knowledge. How I wish I could be part of those scholars and their wisdom?"

"You have become as learned as any in Egypt, my queen."

"Except for you. I marvel at the breadth of your experience and knowledge."

"I am but a humble scholar and your obedient servant."

"Oh, get off it, Akhu. No one is listening out here."

They walked on among flowering trees, the scent almost overpowering.

"Are you happy, Juji?" Akhu said.

"It is not a queen's job to be happy. But, I am pleased at our success. The high priest has been defanged. The Romans are giving us more and more freedom to govern ourselves and seem satisfied with our increase in commerce. Trade is what they want, not to quarter legions far from their real enemies. The people seem to like the desert ideas I have inspired with the return to cool and minimal clothing in this awful heat. It took a while but they seem to accept my freeing of the slaves who now work for wages, fair wages that allow them to raise a family. We have much to do but it is a beginning."

"You did not say if you were happy?"

She looked at him, her eyes watering then closed them as they stood at the edge of a reflection pool.

"I have dreams at night but they are not for a queen."

"Will you tell me?"

She looked at him and shook her head then decided to continue.

"I dream of a child at these breasts. I dream of serving a loved one his evening meal. But, it is not a queen who can have these things. It is only the dream of a young woman of the desert."

"You, of all people, deserve them. We should make these dreams come true."

"How, dear Akhu? How?"

"We find you a suitable mate, a man who will make your dreams come alive."

She looked at him and drew a deep breath.

"I have found him but he does not know I exist."

He frowned, shook his head, and said, "I will tell him of your needs."

"You are such a fool, Akhu, such a fool."

Again he was confused.

"All I want is the best for you," he added.

She took another deep breath and said, "The best stands in front of his queen."

With that, she lowered her head and stared at her bare feet.

"Are you saying ...."

"Akhu, you are truly a fool."

"I have told you there is no one since my sister, Sabra died. But, I did not know."

"And now you know where my heart lives," Juji said. "I would give all this up to return to our flat rock in the sun and lie naked listening to the surf pounding below."

Akhu stood beside her, his hands frozen by his sides, at a complete loss of what to say or do. His

queen, his Juji, had just told him she desired him but
...

Her maid ran up the path toward them yelling at the top of her lungs.

"My queen. Come quickly. There is trouble."

The two of them ran after the maid toward the palace gate.

She sat on her throne as the Roman General Ponticus stood before her.

"The Assyrians have crossed the desert in the Levant and are but a few days from Alexandria. I have but one legion remaining in Egypt because of the wise decision of the Prefect to send them north where they were needed. I am afraid there is little we can do to stop them."

She looked out over the serious faces below where she sat and smiled.

"Is the only way to stop them by fighting a losing battle?"

"What are you saying?" the general asked forgetting the proper way to address the queen.

"I am saying that sometimes diplomacy is better than fighting. But if we must fight we must win."

"I agree but these are barbarians. All they want is to plunder not to conquer or rule."

The Prefect arrived out of breath and stepped up.

"Did I hear correctly as I entered?"

"You did," she said. "What are our other options beside fighting?"

"May I speak," Akhu said coming forward. "If you recall, Prefect, we met long ago and made a decision based on reason, not of a lust for death."

"I do. We spoke of a peace we would share which has worked well for Rome and equally well for Egypt."

"I do not want to put words in our Pharaoh's mouth but what if we approached them and made some kind of compromise. Would it not be better than to see Alexandria sacked once again?"

They all looked at the queen.

"Akhu, take who you wish and go to them, feel them out, and find a way to settle this problem."

He crossed his chest in the Roman salute and backed out of the room.

Chapter Twenty Five - Failed Negotiations

For two days and nights, he rode across the desert toward the Levant and the oncoming Assyrian armies. Beside him rode two trusted men who had been with him since his return to Alexandria, Sampson and John.

Toward dawn on the third day, they approached the Assyrian camp along the ridge of a dry river bed, thousands of conical tents steaming in the morning mist.

"It is huge," young Sampson said as they approached.

Challenged, then led by armed guards, they trotted up to the commander's tent and waited until they were summoned.

"What is an Egyptian doing in my camp?'" the man said in Greek, his voice high and with a slight lisp.

"We come to find out the Assyrian's intentions as you approach our lands?"

"Is it not clear? Look out at those tents filled with brave Assyrian soldiers hungry for conquest."

"Then you come to conquer Egypt as many before you have tried?"

The commander looked at him in surprise, a single Egyptian and two soldiers who had the audacity to ride into his armed camp.

"You tire me. What is it you come for?"

"I come to offer an alternative to death, an alternative to the loss of thousands of men and much of your treasure. We should sit and talk."

"Talk is of no importance here. Men die. That is what war is all about."

"But if we work together as we have done with the Romans, all will benefit and none will die."

"You dare stand in front of me, a man who serves the Romans like a dog, a man who's land has been conquered by a few legions of Roman soldiers? Why should I even listen to this drivel? I have ten thousand eager, hungry men, all waiting for the riches and beautiful women of Egypt."

"Is this what has become of the learned and just Assyrians, a people of great accomplishment, a horde of angry soldiers intent on rape and plunder?"

The commander stood, his hand going to his sword.

"I am not a forgiving man. If you had not come under a flag of truce your head would be dangling from the end of this sword by now."

Akhu, his face red with anger at the failure to turn the mind of the Assyrian, took a deep breath.

"If I have offended you, I apologize but I speak the truth."

"Leave at once and ride fast. I will send ten men after you in one hour."

Akhu nodded and left the tent, beckoning his men to mount and ride out of the camp. They rode at a gallop until they were far from the Assyrians.

Akhu called a halt and spoke to his men.

"Samson, ride night and day until you get to Thebes. Tell them what is about to happen. Tell them Juji and Suffi call them to battle. Get as many men to Alexandria as possible and as fast as they can ride."

"Are these words Juji and Suffi some kind of code?" the soldier asked.

"Yes, they are a code words that will get you prompt action."

"John, you ride to the gypsies and tell Dorian of our need. Tell him his men will receive additional riches. He will understand. Tell him to bring every gypsy from all over the desert. He will know how to do this."

The horses reared and dug their hoofs into the sand as Akhu circled around them on his nervous animal.

"I will ride to the coast and find King Mattu and the Sea People. It is a great risk but one we must take. Now, ride. All of Egypt is counting on you."

Four days later, Akhu rode exhausted through the palace gates. As ordered, the Egyptian army and the lone Roman Legion were in place under the command of General Ponticus. He quickly told the general of his failure to bring sense to the Assyrians and to expect an attack any day. The general, a veteran of many battles, nodded that he understood.

"I have summoned all our friends and some of our recent enemies to help but they may be too late. Unfortunately, the Sea People were raiding the Greeks. They will not know of our problem soon enough."

He nodded and thanked Akhu who rode off to the palace to report to his queen.

Akhu, covered in leather armor, stood at the wall with General Ponticus.

"Do they know there are only four or five thousand of us in the city against that," the general said pointing to the camp of the Assyrians on the East bank of the Nile, a thousand camp fires lighting up the night sky.

"We have no choice but to defend our city to the last man," Akhu said.

"There are more than ten thousand of them, all eager for our heads and our women's bodies. But,

I swear, each of my men will be as good as ten of theirs."

Akhu used to heroic talk such as his, nodded his head and studied the camp in the distance.

"What if we attacked them as they sleep?'

The general looked at him, an astonished expression on his face.

"We either die here in the city and bring its destruction or die out on the edge of the desert," Akhu said. "It may save the city and all who are in it."

The general looked out over the ramparts toward the Assyrian camp. All tents were in a long line along the river bank, stretching as far to the right and left as he could see.

"They are all concentrated on the edge of the Nile," he almost whispered. "There are no reserves held in the rear. It is a thin line everywhere."

He looked at Akhu and smiled.

Akhu, thinking as he spoke, said, "Could we not cross the river on small boats, penetrate their line, attack from behind, confuse them, cause panic when they don't know where their enemy is?"

"You read my mind. But, we must move quickly."

The two rushed down the steps from the rampart where the general spoke rapidly to his men who were used to making last minute changes of plan.

Half the garrison left the gates and plunged silently into the darkness toward the river and the hundreds of fishing boats tied to the West bank. As quietly as possible, they spread out into seven different attacking forces and guided boats loaded with soldiers into the Nile's slow, silt laden current.

Akhu commanded unit five that approached the East bank, his boat a good distance from unit four on his left and unit six, commanded by General Ponticus on his right. At the center of their spread out units, he stood at the bow, sword drawn, waiting for the sound of sand under the keel.

Quietly, he and his men slipped onto solid ground and crawled on their bellies up the slope where they waited for the signal. Only minutes later, a horn sounded and nearly three thousand men raced over the banks and into the sleeping camps of the enemy.

As hoped, each unit quickly pierced the Assyrian line and turned to attack from the rear. The enemy was in total confusion but soon regained order and began a methodical counterattack on each of the seven units of Egyptians and Romans. Though they fought bravely, the defenders of Alexandria fell one by one. Soon, more than half of them were dead, piled up almost like a barrier. Behind their comrades, the living still fought, determined to struggle to the last man.

Akhu's unit was down to thirty men, all standing back to back, slashing at the Assyrians who came in waves, their bodies falling like sheared wheat in front of Akhu's men.

"I fear this is the end," a young boy said to Akhu just as a blade severed his head from his neck.

Akhu brought the attacker down with one thrust of his long sword then faced four more who stood directly in front of him. His thoughts went to Sabra, to Juji and her smile, as sword after sword were deflected until he could barely raise it more than waist high.

A scream rent the air. The Assyrian's turned in panic to face a horde of galloping horses that charged into the battle, cutting Assyrians down like sickles in a flax field. More shouts and men raced out of the night, men with the clothes of gypsies, all swinging swords and knives and forked prongs, men of the desert who knew no fear.

The Assyrians, their line broken in many places, fell back but the Nile offered no retreat. Rapidly they were cut down by hordes if black soldiers wearing the colors of Thebes.

Akhu, bleeding from cuts, leaned on his long sword and turned to congratulate General Ponticus. But, the brave Roman lay on his back, a knife in his throat, his eyes closed in a peace that had finally come after a life of war.

King Odrum of Thebes rode up on his painted horse and smiled down at Akhu.

"We will ride into the city, all of us, and discuss this day over the beer of Alexandria which I hear is among the finest."

A soldier brought a horse and helped Akhu onto its back. With a ragged assembly of gypsies and the soldiers of Thebes, they rode to the river, manned the boats, and entered Alexandria's gates as the light of a new day streamed down on them.

She sat on her throne, her bare arms on the lions and looked out at the men who had saved Alexandria and Egypt.

"I issue a pardon for the Gypsies of the desert who will hopefully accept a great treasure from Egypt."

She then looked out at King Odrum of Thebes who still had on his bloody armor, his black skin covered in sweat.

"I offer you, King Odrum, something we have thought about for many days. Will Thebes join Egypt and bring the Upper Nile into our orbit? Our combined strength plus that of the territories beyond would bring enormous treasure to our lands."

The king, older by fifty years than the young queen sitting before him, smiled, his eyes roaming her body that was free of bindings in a similar way that his women dressed, and wondered.

"We will think on your grand offer. It is possible that a union of a king and a queen could make this happen," he said.

Akhu, having noticed his appreciation of the queen and understanding his meaning, stepped forward.

"I dare not speak for our queen but it has always been our tradition for a queen pharaoh to not marry but to remain a chaste deity. As our pharaoh, she is a god and worshiped by all and not by one."

"But, I am told that Egyptian gods share their bed with mere mortals, even with each other?"

"That is so," she said, "But this queen is different from the others. We will have a treaty, a union of our lands but not of their king and queen. I have much to do and cannot be encumbered by a husband and the children that will follow."

King Odrum shrugged his shoulders, not surprised that his age mattered to such a beautiful woman.

"Let it be so," the king said. "But, such beauty should not be wasted. Do not wait. Take a strong and good man to your bed and bring children as wise as their mother into Egypt."

"Thank you, King Odrum." she said, her appreciative glance toward Akhu not going unnoticed by the king from Thebes.

Chapter Twenty Six - The Crescent Birthmark

Four times each month on the day following the quarters of the moon, the new Pharaoh invited her subjects to stand before her and make a request or complaint that she would consider and possibly grant.

She sat on a simple chair at the far end of the great hall, a huge crowd of Alexandrians standing along the sides. A line of fifty applicants stood in the center, the first approaching her and bowing.

"What is your request?" the queen asked.

For a moment, the man's voice wouldn't come to him standing so close to his queen. He stared at her, his eyes taking in the sight before him, his queen, a god, a beautiful woman dressed in a linen loin cloth and a starched white linen top, a single piece of cloth with a square hole in the center through which her head protruded. The starched cloth hung down from around her neck and ended just below her bare breasts. Never before had there been such a pharaoh. He, as all who stood in the line behind him, had never been so close to a pharaoh much less be asked to speak, to make a request or a complaint.

"My queen," he mumbled.

"Speak up. Do not be afraid."

"My land has been taken by soldiers. It is all I have."

She looked at Akhu who stood at her side.

"It is true," Akhu said. "His land is in the center of the new harbor being built to accommodate the larger ships that arrive in Alexandria."

She looked at the man and said, "You will be given twice the amount of land somewhere of your choosing and a suspension of your taxes for one year."

His face went slack with disbelief as he bowed and backed away nodding his thank you over and over.

The next was a woman of middle years who bowed her head and spoke.

"I have lost my husband in the war with the Assyrians and have no way to feed my four children. Is there not some compassion for the families of those who gave their lives for their pharaoh?"

Juji looked at the woman as tears flowed down her worn and tired face and turned to Akhu.

"Are all those lost accounted for?"

"Yes, your majesty."

"Please see that food and shelter are given to every widow or mother of those who died."

"I will do as you command."

Three more approached and were listened to then sent away satisfied.

She looked into the wicked glare of the high priest who stood in front of her not bowing, his tall, thin body draped in the black cloth of Osiris, the god of the dead.

"What is it you wish, priest," she said in a firm voice.

"I have come to unveil an imposter. I have been told of a deformity that Queen Sabra has that is unique, that is hers alone."

"What are you saying, priest? Out with it," she barked at the top of her voice making everyone in the room turn and listen.

The priest stepped back and looked into the crowd.

"I am here to reveal to you, good people of Alexandria, that your queen is an imposter, that she is the maid,. Juji, not the woman Sabra who the pharaoh made Regent."

A hum of voices rose in the room. Akhu put his hand on the hilt of his sword as the priest turned back to face Juji.

"The second consort, Sabra has a birth mark on her right hip, " he said slapping his hip with the flat of his hand making a cracking sound that startled everyone but the Queen. "You will show us you do not have a birth mark there."

Juji looked at Akhu and back at the priest then stood, the flap of the starched panel bending forward as she rose, exposing her breasts to everyone in the room.

"You dare challenge your queen?" she said in a low venomous voice. "Stand back, priest and listen carefully to what I am about to say."

The room went absolutely quiet.

"I am Queen Sabra, the anointed Regent of Egypt until an heir is born to continue our new dynasty of good will and peace." She stared down at the priest. "You have doubted your queen, your living god, and will pay a dear price for it."

Confident in his claim, the priest smiled.

"By the end of this day, you will no longer be queen." he said.

"Or you will lose your head."

He smiled again and turned to the crowd.

"I have made a request. Will she not prove that she has a birthmark on her hip?"

The people, confused and worried about what was happening, spoke softly but agreed with the priest.

"I do not need their approval," she said stepping forward and reaching for the knot on her loin cloth.

Her hand went under the bottom edge of the cloth and slowly raised it. All eyes stared as more and more of their queen's thigh and hip were laid bare. A gasp went through the crowd as she stopped. A dark, crescent mark, high on her hip, stood out on her perfectly oiled, olive skin.

The priest's face went blank as the stared at the birthmark, his mouth falling open.

"It is a fake, a mark made with henna," the priest shouted rushing forward with a wet cloth in his hand. "I will prove it."

Akhu grabbed his hand before he got close and took the cloth from him.

"Are you afraid? " the priest shouted. "Will you not test the mark?"

Akhu stepped up to Juji and handed her the cloth, looking into her eyes as if to say all is lost.

She took the wet cloth from his hand, and staring into the eyes of the priest, rubbed it against the mark again and again, rubbing hard until the skin around it was red and sore.

Juji lowered her loin cloth back in place and sat again in her chair beckoning for her next subject to approach as two guards led the priest away.

"How? How did you do that?" Akhu asked that evening as he sat by her side, eating a small meal.

She smiled.

"I have told you that I knew everything about your sister, everything. I have been putting a henna mark on my hip for many months and finally decided to have it made permanent with a tattoo. Do you like it as well on me as on her?"

"Yes. You were marvelous. No one will ever doubt you again."

A week passed while Akhu labored in the library with an assistant from Judea, a learned man who he was grooming to run the library. Akhu's position as the pharaoh's chief advisor was taking too much of his time and energy to attend to affairs of state and also run the library.

"I will be back at sunset," he said clasping the man on his shoulder,. "You will be a better chief librarian than either my father or me."

Quickly, he raced to the new harbor where Juji waited on the Queen's barge.

He passed the guards standing on the dock, jumped onto the barge, and pulled the curtain behind him. She sat on a mound of pillows, a cool drink in her hand, wearing the thinnest of linen dresses, one that he had admired long ago.

"You are late. I almost left without you." she said handing him her cup for a refill.

He went to a small table that held a pitcher and poured as the barge moved away from the dock. Towed by twelve slaves pulling at their oars, they dragged the barge out into the current of the Nile.

A tapestry hung behind her, shielding her from the view of the slaves laboring at the oars. But, a cool river breeze flowed over them from the other three open sides that were draped in gauze.

"This is just what a weary body needs," he said lowering himself onto a pile of pillows.

She sipped and looked at him over the top of her cup.

"Is something wrong?" he asked. "You look at me in such a strange way. Have I offended you somehow? If so, it was not my intention to do so."

"No. No. I was just thinking of what we have done."

He took a deep breath and sighed.

"You have become the best pharaoh queen Egypt has ever known. The land prospers. We are fighting no one. The people love you."

"And your Juji is now the god queen of Egypt, loved by all and yet alone, wrapped in her cloak as a goddess."

"Yes, it is the way of queens."

She sighed and looked out at the swift current racing by.

"I feel like the Nile, each day flows by as I grow older and more lonely."

"What are you saying, Juji?"

"That there is no heir to my throne. We have begun a new dynasty and there must be an heir to my throne. Who knows if a crocodile might leap onto this boat and eat me alive?"

"It is why I serve you. That will never happen."

"We are here where no one can listen to what I am about to say. I have chosen you, Akhu. I wish for you to give me that heir."

He looked at her, lying on the mound of pillows, her exquisite body visible through the sheer linen of her dress, a magnificent woman, his queen, his best friend who had saved his life more often than he had saved hers, and shook his head.

"You decline your queen?"

"I cannot. We have spoken of this before. My heart belongs to my sister, Sabra. I cannot abandon that love."

"She is dead, Akhu. I am alive."

He lowered his head and looked into his cup, small leaves swirling around in the liquid, a hundred thoughts moving in a less orderly way than the tea leaves. He looked up to say something more and froze.

She stood naked, her torn dress thrown onto the pillows, severed from her body by a dagger she held at her throat. Her oiled body glistened and shinned in the bright light filtering into the barge through the mesh curtains.

"Would you have me die an unsatisfied woman?" she whispered.

"Juji, please. You know how I care for you. I love you like no one else."

"Then prove your love now. Take your Queen."

She stepped forward, dropped the dagger, and reached for the top of his loin cloth. A smile crossed her face as she pulled the knot and let it fall at his feet.

Akhu lay back, covered in sweat, his heart pounding, and smiled up at the roof of the Queen's barge. She sat at his feet, legs tucked under her naked body, massaging his toes one by one, her warm fingers slowly reviving him.

"By all the gods, I have never..."

"There is more, dear Akhu," she said moving over his body.

For five days, the queen begged forgiveness and privacy from her servants, even the pleas of her sister, Janis, saying a sickness kept her in bed. For five days, she retrieved and ate meals placed outside her chamber door. For five nights and days, she and Akhu learned all there was to know about each other until, exhausted, he stood above her, looking down at the woman who had freed his soul, and smiled.

"You and Sabra are now one," he said taking her outstretched hand and pulling her to her feet.

She folded into his arms.

"I never want this to end, however, it must. You will move into my chambers but we must get back to running my country."

He smiled and gave her the Roman salute, slapping his arm across his bare chest.

Chapter Twenty Seven - Bridget, the Celt

A week later, they took an evening stroll in the city, Juji dressed as a commoner so she would not be recognized.

"I love being out like this. It is like it was before my becoming queen."

They walked down a lonely street toward the new harbor, Akhu having promised to show her the huge ship that had arrived from Rome that day. On the dock, he pointed to the sails, massive and rolled up on spars horizontal to the masts.

"They have no idea how much faster our Lateen sails would make them," he said.

"What do we have here," a rough voice sounded from behind where they stood looking at the ship.

A man wearing a leather jacket and breeches above shining black boots, strode toward them followed by two tough looking men similarly dressed. A young woman with blonde hair walked slowly behind them.

"A beauty such as you should not be in a place like this," he said coming up and leering at Juji's open topped gown, her breasts all but exposed as was the style in Egypt now.

His two men stood back and laughed. The girl cowered behind him.

"Where I come from, a wench like you is fair game. Winner takes all."

"Stand aside," Akhu said laying his hand on the hilt of his sword.

The man looked at his two ruffians and nodded. Immediately, they drew their swords and rushed Akhu.

Juji heard the clanging of blades and gave their leader a swift kick in the shin. He let out a howl and grabbed her around the throat. Almost as suddenly, the blonde woman drove a small dagger into his back and, screaming obscenities in some foreign language, dragged it back and forth opening his shoulder wide. A current of blood shot out as he dropped to the ground.

Juji turned just as Akhu drove his long sword into the heart of the second and last man, withdrew it, and stood over the dying man.

The blond woman fell to her knees, her long dress soiling in the mud of a puddle, tears pouring down her face.

"I am sorry, Madam, but he attacked us," Akhu said.

The woman looked up. Akhu saw she was a young girl, beautiful, but strangely with a smile on her pretty face.

"You have done a great service to me. Thank you both." she said standing, her dress and small jacket a mess from the mud.

Juji looked at Akhu and then at the young girl and said, "What will you do now?"

"I am from the north, beyond Rome, the wild country of the Celts they call it. I have been his slave for a month or more. I do not know."

Juji took her hand.

"You will come with us. I will see that no more harm comes to you."

The three of them moved quickly back the way Juji and Akhu had come, back along the lane toward the palace.

"You have no idea how awful that man is... was," the blond girl said. "He did unspeakable things to me."

"You are safe now. What shall I call you?"

The girl hesitated for a moment then said, "I am called, Bridget. But who do I thank?"

Juji looked at her as they approached the palace.

"I am Queen Sabra of Egypt and this is my trusted advisor, Akhu, a very learned man."

The girl stopped in her tracks and stared at her.

"A queen out walking on the docks?"

"Yes, a queen must see her city as others see it. Good government cannot be done from a throne room."

Bridget bowed her head and said, "I owe you my life and pledge it to you. Please accept what little I can offer."

"I accept that, Bridget. You will be by my side. I was once in your shoes."

"But, you are a queen."

Juji hooked her arm under the girl's and whispered, "Not everything is as it seems."

Akhu following behind, stared at his Queen, his Juji who had more kindness in her lovely body than all of Alexandria combined.

Bridget, eyes wide in amazement at the sudden turn of events, sat on a stool in the queen's bed chamber. Juji, who had changed into an all but transparent linen gown, open at the top, stood at the far end of the room holding up a similar dress.

"You must get out of those muddy, awful clothes that are not fitting for a young woman. Here, try this on for size as we are very close in height."

Bridget stood, nervously fingering a button at the top of her jacket.

"Go ahead," Juji said smiling. "You will soon get used to our customs."

Bridget undid the buttons, one at a time, and removed her wet jacket. Beneath was a long, wool dress buttoned in the back, closed at the breast, and topped by a small bit of soiled lace. Juji nodded that she should continue.

More buttons were undone and the dress dropped to the floor. Bridget stood in front of the queen in a white under shirt and bloomers.

"By the gods, who invented such tortures? Remove everything or die in the heat of Egypt," she said laughing.

The girl removed her under shirt, well developed young breasts open to the air for possibly the first time, and hesitated.

"All of it," Juji whispered.

The bloomers fell to the floor and Bridget stood in front of the queen, stark naked. But what Juji saw was an incredibly beautiful, young girl, pale skin, freckles on her face, hair like spun gold.

"I will bet this is the first time another woman has ever seen you naked. Am I right?"

"Yes, your majesty."

"And only a few men?"

"Only the one who fell to Master Akhu's sword."

Juji brought the linen dress to her and held it up.

"Put this on and we shall see."

Bridget pulled it over her head and smoothed it down on her hips.

"But, you can see right through it. I would be mortified in public."

Juji smiled and spread the top so her breasts showed.

"Many women including me wear nothing on top if we wish. It is very different now in Egypt, much like it was two centuries ago when women enjoyed a great amount of freedom. I intend to bring back that freedom and more."

A knock on the door announced Akhu who entered and stood in front of them, his eyes wide and staring.

"What have you done to this poor girl?" he asked looking her up and down. "I have never seen such a transformation in my life. She arrives like a waif and in only hours looks like a goddess."

"Thank you, Master Akhu but I am not sure I am ready for such immodesty?"

"You must not worry. Ju... Queen Sabra will guide you and teach you. It is quite customary in Egypt and makes sense because of our extreme heat."

"Or in the lust we see in men's eyes," Juji said taking his hand. "I will have Bridget as my personal maid. Akhu. Get used to seeing her at all times."

He remembered how Juji always stood in the shadows as he made love to Sabra, how she waited on him when he was in her quarters, how she listened and learned. It didn't slip by his thoughts that Bridget would be in the same shadows as Juji had once been. Maybe that is why his queen had taken such a liking to her?

Juji held his hand and looked over at her creation.

"So, do you like what we have done?"

"I like whatever you do, whenever you do it," he said kissing the hand that held his.

"I will leave you two," Bridget said moving toward the door.

"No, Bridget. You don't understand. You will be at my side at all times. I will take my Akhu to bed but you will remain in my chambers."

She reddened and bowed her head.

"No more of that either," Juji said. "You are free as of now. All the servants are free and receive a monthly stipend. Yours will be two gold coins. What I ask of my staff is absolute loyalty. That's all."

"Free. Do you mean that? I don't know what to say?"

"Retire to the shadows. I will reduce my Akhu to a worn out man before the moon comes out."

Bridget soon became a sensation at court, her blond hair causing much comment and received noticeable envy among the other women. With Juji's guidance she had learned to use kohl to blacken her eyelids and henna on her lips and cheeks.

Slowly, she became more and more accustomed to the minimal clothing of the Egyptians, even to the point where she served Akhu and Juji in the chambers bare to the waist.

"You are a lovely girl," Akhu said.

"Thank you, master Akhu. I am finding it much easier now. Mistress Sabra has taught me a great deal in the past week."

"Tell me, Bridget, why was the foreigner in Alexandria?"

She paled at the mention of him but took a deep breath.

"I overheard many things, much of which I did not understand."

"Things like what?"

"I come from a land far to the west of Rome. It is a raw and uncivilized land filled with warring tribes, a fertile land that stretches from the Mediterranean Sea to high mountains called the Alps."

Akhu nodded having read of such barbarians in his library.

"All the tribes know how to do is fight and kill. They live like animals not like we do here. My father led a band of men in the land of the Celts. He was killed in a fierce battle. My mother, my two sisters, and I were taken as slaves."

"That man?"

"Yes, he pulled me from a muddy, cattle stall where we were kept and took me to his home, a cold, stone building with a thatch roof that leaked when it rained. Though he had little, his dreams were great. For the next month, we traveled throughout the land as he spoke to one tribal leader after another preaching unity and conquest."

"Is that why he came here?"

"I heard him say many times that Alexandria was the richest plum in the world and easy to conquer. His message rang true with many and, as of now, there are a thousand ships on the Celtic coast waiting for men to assemble for an attack on Alexandria."

"And that is why he was here, scouting out the harbor?"

"Yes, I am afraid that is so."

Akhu leaned back on his pillows and drew a deep breath.

"My queen. From what I have read these barbarians have no interest in colonizing like the Romans and Greeks. All they want is plunder, rape, and the spoils of war. Bridget has confirmed this and I fear we are in for another, and far worse, invasion, one of bloodthirsty animals not wise men who sometimes make room for reason."

"What do you suggest, Akhu. I will listen."

"I propose we spend much of our treasury on building our army to defend Egypt. Our new allies in Thebes and the Gypsy hoards will come if we make it worth their effort. The Sea People may or may not join us depending on where their ambition is focused at this time."

"The man said there would be ten thousand soldiers on the ships," Bridget said.

"And Egypt has less than four thousand plus another thousand from our allies. It is another uneven battle," Akhu said.

"We have the gods on our side," Juji said taking his damp hand, a feeling of dread passing through her as she felt his pain.

Chapter Twenty Eight - The Battle Off Sicily

Akhu sat with the generals, a map of the Mediterranean spread out before them.

"If we could choose the place of battle, the odds would be better," said young Sampson who had risen rapidly to general since his bravery in the war with the Assyrians.

An older man with scars on his arm, reached out and poked a finger at the map.

"We might march our troops out into the western desert and draw them ashore far west of Alexandria, fight them in the sand where they have no experience?"

Akhu leaned back, his hand under his chin, rubbing the stubble of his unshaven face.

"When will they come?" he asked.

"If the woman, Bridget's, information is correct, a month would be my guess"

"We cannot guess. We must know," Akhu said. "If they wait another month, the Mediterranean will be rough. What if we fought them at sea where they have zero experience and will probably be sick and terrified."

The men looked from one to the other, young Sampson nodding his head that he thought it a good idea.

"The Romans will let our fleet anchor on their west coast," the young man said. "We could wait there until our spies tell us they approach We can make a surprise attack. They will be ill prepared for such a daring thing."

All the men nodded.

"Send spies to watch them," Akhu said. "I will go to the Sea People and tell them of our plan. Let us hope they will join us as we have far too few ships for such an endeavor."

She lay back in his arms as he kissed her hair, his hands still on her damp body.

"In your bed, I am a different man from the warrior who prepares to leave these warm arms to do battle with barbarians."

"You must go and return victorious for I have news." Juji said.

He looked into her wet eyes, a smile on her lovely face.

"What is it?"

"You will once again father an heir to the throne of Egypt but this time he will be born, raised to be a king, and rule justly and wisely."

He smothered her with kisses, mumbling, "By the grace of Isis, thank you. Thank you, my love."

"Return safely. We will marry and then raise our son."

Bridget, in the shadows of the room, drew a deep breath as her fears for his life were justified by what she knew of the men he would soon face.

Akhu stood on the deck of King Mattu's command ship, a vessel of twelve sails, half lateen rigged for heading closer to the wind.

"It is a wonderful ship, King Mattu. One Eye would have marveled at such a thing."

"You bring up our old friend for a reason, is that not so?"

"Yes, sir. I do. Alexandria is once again threatened by her enemies but this time it is not one we know."

"Who are they?"

"The Barbarians from far west of Rome. They come with ten thousand wild men from the forests of the north. The stories that have reached my ears are those of brutality and killings such as we have never seen before."

"And you wish my help?"

"You saw the riches our Queen gave those who helped us defeat the Assyrians?'

"She was most generous."

"If your ships will carry us to battle, I will guarantee far greater riches will fall into your hands."

"And if we lose?"

"All the southern countries will fall with us and the animals will devour us."

King Mattu stroked his graying beard and nodded.

"I cannot risk all on one venture such as this. I am sorry, Akhu. You must make this your battle alone."

Akhu clasped his hand in his and whispered, "The god Atem wakened me two nights in a row and spoke to me. He has told me you will not live more than a month more. Is this true, Mattu?"

The old man drew a deep breath and nodded yes.

"I spit up blood and feel pain in my chest."

"Will you come to Alexandria and let our surgeons examine you? They are the world's best. We can be there in two days on your fast ship."

"I still say no."

Akhu said that he understood and stepped back as King Mattu gave the order to set sail for Alexandria.

"A bleeding ulcer," the surgeon said. "It can be cured with diet and a potion of ground sea shells."

Akhu thanked him and went to the room where King Mattu was folding his tunic across his massive chest.

"My surgeon will cure you on one condition, that your fleet join ours in this task. The queen wishes you to come to the palace to place the promised treasure in your hands."

"If this is so, I will follow you to the ends of the earth. I will live," he shouted and clapped Akhu on the back with the flat of his broad hand.

She placed a gold plate heaped with jewels on the lap of King Mattu who looked at it, smiled and reached for his cup of wine.

"No, you must not. Remember what the surgeon said," Akhu admonished.

The king withdrew his hand and picked up a ruby the size of an egg.

"Where did such riches come from if I may ask?"

"These are the stones of Nubia gained by the bloodied hands of brave Egyptian warriors long ago. They are now the rewards of another brave man, King Mattu," Juji said standing beside him and smiling down at where he sat.

He looked up, his eyes wandering over her mostly exposed body and said, "If this is the way you live, Akhu, I may give up the sea and take a woman."

A week passed as the hastily assembled fleet roared west on a strong Mediterranean wind, five hundred ships filled with armed men.

King Mattu, Akhu, and the generals sat in a cabin on the command ship, a map of the Mediterranean spread out on a low table.

Young general, Sampson, the one who had suggested such a bold move, pointed at the coast of the Celts.

"We know almost nothing about this part of the world and I have been told the Romans have seldom ventured there either. We will be at a disadvantage if we engage their fleet there." He looked at Akhu. "Have you decided where we will surprise them?"

Akhu leaned over the map.

"I have spoken at length with Bridget who has a keen eye for these things. She has told me much about the habits and battles the Celts have fought in the past. If they are like other people they will follow what they know best."

"But they are not like others," another officer said, "They are more like animals."

Akhu nodded that he agreed.

"Therefore, we must be smarter and more cunning. An attacking fleet trying to reach Alexandria must sail through here," he said pointing to where the Mediterranean narrowed between the southern coast of Sicily and the north coast of Africa. "It is wide and they could slip by without notice but their fleet is huge and their ships cumbersome according to Bridget. We will follow our plan and hide our fleet in the vast Sicilian harbor of Marsala. As you see, we will be upwind and can strike when they pass by."

"But if we miss them there will be nothing between them and Alexandria. All will be lost without bending a sword," another said.

Akhu looked at him, noting his timidness and went on.

"We will have a dozen small sailing vessels disguised as fishing boats crisscrossing the straits. Not a single ship will elude us much less a fleet of five hundred."

The young man's face reddened but Akhu patted him on the shoulder.

"The gods will guide us, young man."

Another hour was spent discussing tactics and strategy as Akhu listened to the veteran Sea People and his generals fine tune the plan.

As the meeting came to a close, Akhu pulled young general Sampson aside.

"I have taken the liberty to have the Celt, Bridget, disguised as a man and in my cabin below. She knows these people better than all of us put together and may be of invaluable help."

"But, sir, a woman on board a fighting ship filled with armed men?"

"She is disguised and looks like a cabin boy. Please guard her with your life. Your queen and I put her in your hands to protect."

He slapped his arm across his chest and nodded that he would do so.

"Come, I will show you," Akhu said leading him down the steps of the command ship toward his cabin.

They entered the small room to find Bridget standing with her back to them and buttoning up a cotton shirt.

She turned but not before they saw what she was doing, tucking the ends of a wide strap of linen into the tight folds around her breasts.

"I must not look like a woman," she said standing straight and facing them.

"This is General Sampson, Bridget. He has pledged to guard you with his life."

Sampson came forward and bowed his head, his eyes not leaving hers, a pounding in his chest that was unfamiliar.

"You need not bow as to a slave," Bridget said.

"Ah, but Akhu tells me you are no longer a slave but a favorite of the queen. I am honored to stand at your side."

She smiled and couldn't help but notice how his eyes bored into hers.

"Bridget, you will go with Sampson as his valet, but be available if I should need your help."

She looked at Sampson who stared at her, a dampness on his brow, and smiling.

"I will do as you wish, Master Akhu," then followed the general out of the cabin and down the passageway.

The Egyptian fleet lay at anchor in the huge harbor at Marsala, Sicily, shielded from view by a high peninsula of land that arched out from the mainland to an opening that led to the sea beyond. Nine small fishing boats had left and were patrolling the straits.

General Sampson, his valet by his side, stood at the rail of the command ship as Akhu approached.

"We are ready," Akhu said.

Sampson held his hand up and said, "I do not like what the wind in doing. It is shifting to the west. If it moves more it will come directly through the harbor entrance and we will not be able to leave for open water. It will be right on our nose."

Akhu wet his finger and held it up.

"You are right. Do you have a suggestion?"

"We cannot put to sea or surprise will be lost. If we stay, we might be trapped here by the wind and they will sail past on an open road to Alexandria. I do not know what the best choice is?"

"The season of the north winds approaches," Bridget said. "The wind then will be strong and always from the north, a favorable wind for us."

"But it shifts to the west," Sampson said looking at her standing next to him in her man's clothes.

"It will become from the north. It always does. It always will."

Sampson looked at Akhu.

"This is why we have her at our side, Akhu said. "She knows these waters. We should listen to her and trust the gods to send us a favorable wind."

Sampson nodded and left, Bridget following a few feet behind as Akhu wondered at his young general's odd behavior.

Two days passed, the wind continued to shift from north to west and back again adding to the nervousness of the officers.

Bridget again assured him that, once the season was upon them, the wind would come from the north and be very strong.

He knocked on Sampson's cabin door, heard voices, then the door opened slowly and Samson peeked out.

"Sir, you surprised me," he said pulling a sleeping gown over his bare body.

"The wind rises and the ships strain at their anchors. We must ready ourselves."

"A moment," he said but not before Akhu had stepped into the cabin.

Bridget lay on his bed naked and reaching for her clothes.

"I am sorry, sir but..." Sampson choked out.

"She is a good woman. Do not be sorry." Akhu said.

Sampson, feeling relieved, looked at her and said," Thank you for what you have given me. I am now ready to fight."

Akhu smiled remembering and wishing nights of passion were his again.

"One of our scouts reports the Celt fleet approaches the straits. We must move quickly." Akhu said turning to leave.

Akhu and Sampson were followed by Bridget who pulled her clothes on as they rushed toward the steps to the deck above.

"The wind is very strong," Sampson said when they stepped out on deck.

Men rushed by, sailors readying the ship for raising anchor and armed soldiers buckling on breast plates and sheathing freshly sharpened swords.

The captain, standing on the bridge above them gave the order to break out the sails and raise anchor. Followed by the rest of the fleet, the helmsman steered them out of the harbor and into crashing waves.

Bridget tugged at Sampson's arm and shouted above the howling wind.

"It is what we call a Meltami, a fierce north wind of great strength."

The three of them stood at the rail, Akhu and Sampson armed and ready, Bridget holding a dagger in her clasped hand, ready to pay them back for what they had done to her.

Lining the rail were a hundred armed men all soaked to the skin from the pouring rain.

"We will never find them in this weather," Sampson said.

"They will come to us," Bridget said. "Master Akhu, we should stay close to the shore, close to the land with the wind at our back. They will come this way to head into the wind and not be driven onto the shores of Africa."

"How do you know so much about the sea?" Sampson asked.

"She smiled and said, "I was raised in a fishing village and spent many happy days on a small boat. I know this sea like my sister."

Akhu looked up at the sails above, straining in the wind and nodded that he agreed.

"Tell the captain to keep the fleet close to the shore line with the wind at our back. We will wait for them to come."

Sampson ran off to the bridge. Immediately, flags sent the message to the fleet that turned as one and headed east along the Sicilian coast line.

Akhu looked at Bridget, soaked to the skin and looking too much like a woman in her man's clothing.

"Have you taken my general's heart?"

"He is a good man and finds this poor girl with blond hair to his liking."

"Queen Sabra will be pleased that you have found a lover."

Bridget smiled and watched as the general came rushing back to her side.

"The captain says it is a good plan. We will be upwind of them when they approach, hard pressed and unable to maneuver as we can. He has dispatched half the fleet to run ahead and the rest of us to remain in this area in the hope that they will arrive between our two flanks."

"He plans like a field general. Fighting at sea is much the same I think," Akhu said but did not fail to notice the dagger clutched in Bridget's hand.

"You will not fight, young lady. It is a man's job," Akhu said.

"I will fight. This dagger will bring down as many barbarian rapists as my arm can stab and if all comes to an end, it will plunge into my heart. I will never be taken like that again."

Akhu clasped her on the shoulder letting her know she could fight by Sampson's side.

A lookout shouted from the top of the mast, his voice carried off by the wind.

"He says he sees sails," Sampson said unleashing his sword.

"It begins," Akhu all but whispered and turned to be with his men.

Hard pressed and plunging into heavy seas, a dozen full rigged ships appeared out of a curtain of blowing rain. All were under too much sail, heeling over, sheets of water crashing over their bows and sweeping along their decks.

As they watched them approach, dozens more appeared out of the gloom. Lightning flashed and thunder boomed as the enormous fleet raced toward them.

Akhu waved to the captain above, who ordered the helmsman to turn and engage the oncoming fleet. All two hundred fifty Egyptian ships followed the command ship and raced headlong at the Celts. In but a few minutes, all of the Egyptian ships had thrown grappling hooks on the surprised Celts, boarded them and were engaged in hand to hand ferocious fighting. The other half of the Egyptian fleet attacked from the other side.

Sampson and Akhu along with fifty yelling men boarded what looked to him like the lead ship. Shoulder to shoulder, they hacked their way toward the bridge where an enormous man stood, naked to the waist, rain running down his muscled body, his long, yellow hair and beard soaked, making him look like some evil god.

Akhu raced up the ladder and, with his sword held high, faced this giant Celt who stood, legs planted wide apart, a short sword in each hand.

Below, much of the fighting was ending as the Celts had been caught totally unaware of the danger awaiting them and didn't have time to fight as an organized unit, easy victims for the well trained Egyptians.

The two men faced each other, swords drawn.

"It is over," Akhu said. "Put down your swords."

The man howled in his language and lunged toward Akhu, slashing with both swords and backing Akhu toward the rail. First, he cut his arm then raised the other short sword high. Akhu ducked to the left, as a dagger whished through the air and plunged deep between the Celt's eye. The man looked startled, then his knees buckled and he dropped to the deck, his eyes looking at a young boy standing at the ladder. Seconds later, he toppled onto his face.

Akhu turned, and holding his bleeding arm, nodded his appreciation to Bridget.

"You are an Egyptian now. Thank you," he shouted above the sound of battle below.

She turned and raced down the ladder to be at the side of Sampson who was fighting two hairy men.

Chapter Twenty Nine - Royal Births

Juji kissed her over and over, holding her tight and weeping into her long, blond hair.

"I owe you my life for saving him," Juji said through her tears.

"I only did what had to be done," Bridget said, uncomfortable in her queen's arms and the large belly that pressed against her.

"The child, is it well?" Bridget asked stepping back.

"You may touch it and feel the little prince move about in his eagerness to rule."

Bridget felt what must have been the new king's head.

"He moves. I can feel it."

Juji smiled and kissed her friend again.

"A time will come for you. Just look how long I waited for Akhu to notice and take me in his arms?"

"I may have met that man," Bridget said, "But he is Egyptian and will not want a hated Celtic in his bed."

"Who? Tell me. I will make it so." Juji said looking into her eyes. "What is it, dear Bridget? You may tell me."

The queen leaned back then a knowing smile came to her face, "You may not fool me. Tell me at once. Are you...?"

"Yes, my queen. I hope it does not offend you that I have done this?"

"No. No. I am pleased for you. Our children will be close. My son will play with your child. They will grow up together. Oh, this is wonderful."

"I only hope it pleases the gods."

"Have you embraced one of our gods?"

"Yes, I pay homage to Isis, the fertility and mother goddess who you have shown me is in control of our lives."

"You are a wise girl, wise for your age. I will see that, no matter what the future brings, that you are made wealthy and happy."

"Thank you, mistress. But, I am your servant always."

Juji whispered, "Yet my friend above all other things."

The queen smiled and hugged her friend to her swollen breast.

Juji and Akhu walked in the courtyard of the palace. He held her arm to guide her unsteady feet.

"We must wait no longer, Akhu. I have arranged for a simple ceremony. We will marry tomorrow. I wish for you to be a king for our son to look up to."

He kissed her hand and smiled.

"This will make our lives perfect," he said. "I can hardly wait to sleep with my wife at my side."

They wandered down the path until she tired and he led her back to her chambers.

"I will announce our betrothal to all," he said closing the door and letting her rest.

Bridget rubbed her back with a sponge, the water flowing down into the bathing pool.

"You will be a married queen tomorrow," Bridget said in a sad voice.

"Are you not happy for me?" Juji said looking up at her and taking her hand. "Of all people, I wish for your blessing."

"Of course, mistress. I am most happy for you. It is just that marriage is such a big thing for an Egyptian I am told. Those who marry must be true only to their mate and not be with others. Is that not so?"

"Yes, that is correct but a royal family can do as it wishes. I, however, have no interest beyond my Akhu and never will."

"You are a good woman, mistress, a good woman."

"But," Juji asked in a soft voice, "you said you had your eyes on an Egyptian. Has he noticed your interest? Could he be a father to your child?"

"He is no longer of interest to me but thank you for asking."

"Bridget, just look at you, a slave when you came, a young girl looking like something a camel would not let on its back, and you have developed and grown so much. Just look at how your body has blossomed. I am convinced you will soon be the most beautiful and desirable girl in my court."

"None could be more so than you."

Juji looked down at her swollen belly and sighed.

"It will be a long wait for that to happen."

A hundred of her innermost circle gathered in the throne room where two massive chairs now sat at the end of the room, identical even to the carved lions on the arms. On them sat Akhu and an extremely pregnant, Queen Sabra, she in a gown of woven gold threads that flowed over her like water. Akhu wore a gold tunic and looked very uncomfortable.

The young priest of the god, Horus, stood before them and spoke in ancient Egyptian, passed the gold scepter over his head then hers and pronounced them married.

Juji, as Queen Sabra, reached over and slipped the coiled gold serpent over his wrist and up his arm, the recognized symbol of an Egyptian king. She then touched the Ankh, the oval and cross, to her lips and touched it softly to his shoulder.

All recognized that Sabra would remain pharaoh but have a king at her side. When the boy heir was eight years old, the child would become the new pharaoh.

Bridget stood behind their thrones, hand on her full belly, watching as they married. On completion, Akhu took his queen's hand and led her past the court, nodding to congratulations, giving a wink to young, Janis, and wishing for the peace and quiet of their bed chamber.

Bridget followed carrying the symbols of the pharaoh and king. Bells rang throughout the city and the population celebrated while Akhu and Sabra consummated the marriage in a most compromised position.

"We grow large together," Juji said softly patting Bridget's swollen belly, "How I wish I carried my child as you do. From behind you look absolutely normal where I look like some pregnant camel."

"That is not so, my queen. You look absolutely radiant."

"Is it not thrilling that both of our children will be born in the month of Isis."

Juji sat in the bathing pool as Bridget sponged her back with warm water, dripping it slowly over her olive skin and watching the rivulets flow down and trickle into the pool.

"Your fingers are perfect, Bridget," she said looking up at the lovely, blonde girl who bathed her so expertly. "Sometimes the hands of a woman are as exciting as those of a man."

"It pleases me you feel that way," Bridget said massaging her back.

"Have you ever thought of it?"

""Only when with you, my queen."

"We should not speak this way. It disturbs me but you must know how much I love you."

"And I you."

Juji stood, the water running off her body and let Bridget pat her dry.

"Your robe," Bridget said draping it over the Queen's shoulders.

The last month of their pregnancy passed with both women spending much of their time together in seclusion, taking care that their unborn children suffered nothing but peace and quiet as their times grew close.

The bond of friendship grew as they talked endlessly about their very separate but similar lives. Akhu often sat with them and enjoyed listening to their tales.

"Queen Sabra and I were half sister and brother," Akhu said at Bridget's urging for him to tell about how he and the queen grew up. "We were inseparable as children just as your sons will be. That is until we were captured and Sabra taken away from me into slavery. We were very close."

Bridget had watched the queen's eyes as he spoke and saw them water when he spoke of those times with so much love. She turned and spoke in a low voice to Akhu.

"Why do you say the word 'was' when you speak the name Sabra?"

Akhu reddened in the cheeks and corrected himself, "It was a long time ago."

Bridget looked back at the queen who had drawn a deep breath and bitten at her lip.

"I will say nothing more about it," Bridget said.

Bridget gave birth to a boy child in the privacy of her rooms, nursing it every few hours, and leaving it in the care of her most trusted servant while she attended her queen. It had been decided that her child would be kept secret until after the queen gave birth so as not to overshadow the biggest event in all of Egypt when the heir to the throne was born.

Bridget and the queen walked in the wooded grove of trees at the far end of the courtyard, a place of privacy, cool and open to the sea and a soft breeze. Both wore robes that hung from their shoulders, open in front, Juji's vast expanse of belly protruding and glistening in the sunlight, Bridget's swollen breasts leaking milk

"I must return soon as my breasts tell me it is time to feed my son, Cameron."

"What a lovely name," Juji said.

"It is Celt, a name my family has had for ages."

They sat side by side on a stone bench letting the cool breeze wash over them.

"Just a few moments more," Juji said then grabbed Bridget's arm.

"He comes," she whispered as water flowed down her bare legs.

Bridget stood and helped her queen to her feet.

"I cannot. It comes now," Juji cried in pain and sat back down on the bench. "Run and get help."

Bridget held her arm and watched as the queen lay back, a part of the baby already showing. She removed her robe, folded it, and placed it under the queen's head.

"Lay back. I will do it. I have done this when my sisters were born."

She pushed Juji's knees up and reached for the baby only to find the part showing wasn't the child's head but the crook of its arm.

Through tears, she leaned over her ashen faced queen and whispered. "It is coming out wrong. I will try but it will be bad."

"Bring the pharaoh into this world, Bridget. I can take the pain."

Bridget reached down, fingers probing, reaching inside, holding onto a slippery part of the baby on one side with her fingers and grasping the extended elbow with the other hand.

"Hold on. I will pull now."

She tried to turn the child, blood flowing onto her elbows, Juji screaming in pain, the child moving slowly as she rolled it over inside Juji. Finally, grasping its head with both hands, she pulled as Juji screamed, the child finally bursting free and letting out a fierce cry.

"It is a girl, a beautiful girl," Bridget whispered to the pain streaked face of Juji staring blankly up at her.

Running feet came down the path. Juji was swept up in Akhu's arms and carried back to the palace bed chamber, Juji clutching at his neck, crying in pain.

Bridget and Akhu stood at her bedside, Akhu holding her hand and looking down at their queen's pale face.

"It is a beautiful girl. She has your eyes and lovely hands," he said.

Juji squeezed his fingers with all the strength she had and whispered, "Love her for me," and closed her eyes.

"She has lost too much blood," Bridget whispered..

"No. No." Akhu shouted. "Not again. Not again."

He stayed until her hand grew cold, stood with tears in his eyes and looked at Bridget who held the child to her breast and fed his baby girl with her own milk.

As tears ran down his face, Bridget took his hand and said in a firm voice, "It must be done quickly. She is gone. There is no way to bring her back. But she must live on through a child."

"What are you talking about. It is a girl and will not be acknowledged as the heir," Akhu said through his tears.

"No. A boy will ascend to the throne when he is eight just as planned. Take her baby girl from my hands and wait for my return. We can do this thing."

She handed Juji's baby girl to Akhu whose tears fell on its bloody body, held it close until Bridget returned with her child in her arms.

"Give me Juji's girl," Bridget said taking it from his arms and putting the newborn child in a crib. "Take my Cameron and raise him as the heir."

Akhu stared at her, stunned by her words, looking from one child to the other.

"There is no other way," Bridget said. "I will nurse them both but you are to present my Cameron to the court as the queen's child, the heir. No questions will ever be asked. He even has your black hair and blue eyes."

Akhu, still stunned by what she said, took a long minute to think through his grief, wade through the misery in his head, and realized that it would be for the best. He took Bridget's boy child and walked out the door to face the waiting members of the court, to present an heir to the dynasty begun by their dead Queen, Sabra.

Chapter Thirty - An Heir to the Kingdom

Akhu suffered in silence, working night and day planning the entombment of Juji, the queen know to all as Sabra. She would be put in a modest tomb she had created some time ago. In keeping with her style, she was prepared by the young priest of Horus and, with great ceremony, sealed for eternity within a stone chamber in the Valley of the Dead. Akhu spared her sister, Janis, who begged to be buried in the tomb beside her.

As King, with the heir at his side, Akhu ruled Egypt as wisely as Juji had. Bridget, nursing both children, blossomed into the fairest looking woman in all of Africa, a woman admired by all for her great beauty, perfect body, and absolutely unique blond hair..

The switching of the children at birth was known by no one but Akhu and Bridget. The babies were raised like sister and brother just as he had been with Sabra so many years ago.

They sat under some trees looking out at the sea, the heir at her breast, the girl child in a shaded crib.

"Have you not wondered how much my Cameron looks like an Egyptian and not a fair haired, Celt?" Bridget whispered looking down at the child she had delivered.

Akhu looked away, fearing this conversation.

"Do not be sad. I am not," she said. "What we did on the ship has brought you a son."

"By the gods, Bridget. I did not think at the time. I am sorry. I was weak and took advantage of you."

"You say you are sorry? Is that truly how you feel? When you saw me unbinding my breasts on the ship, did you not feel what I felt? I wanted you then and I still do. Please do not say it was wrong."

He nodded though his thoughts were confused.

"But it brought you a son," she said. "Do you not see? It is as you have told me with you and your beloved, Sabra or Juji. Both of these children are yours but with different mothers. These two babies will grow to love each other as you did with Sabra."

"Are you certain, Bridget. It could have been the Celt who violated you when you were a slave or the Egyptian that you told Juji you favored which I have found to be Sampson."

"I didn't dare tell her that the Egyptian I favored was you and that the child in my belly was yours."

Akhu looked down at his sandals and scuffed the dirt, deep in thought.

"Akhu, think about what I am about to say in a wise and calm way," she said. "The heir you put in Sabra, some years ago, died with her and the throne nearly went to those who had profit and greed in their heads instead of the good people of Egypt. What we did by switching my son, Cameron, with

Juji's daughter was to give Egypt an male heir that will allow you, as king, to raise him as a just and good pharaoh. It was the right thing to do."

"You just said Juji and, as I recall, said it once before. How do you.. .? Where did you hear that name?"

"She told me everything, how she looked so much like Sabra, the queen, that she became her and took her place when she died. It is Sabra in the tomb with the pharaoh Nebrunef, is that not true, Akhu?"

Akhu took a deep breath, nodding yes.

"She told you how we made her queen?" he asked.

"Yes, dear Akhu. Do not look so distressed. It is all right."

"The gods toy with me," he said sighing deeply. "I have lost both of the mothers of my sons."

"What about the black slave, Suffi? You lost her too."

"She told you about her as well?"

"Of course. We were like sisters, the Queen and I. Tell me about this Suffi?"

He realized that there could be no secrets between them and told her about Suffi, the black slave princess, a great friend and companion that had died as well.

"You have loved and lost much," Bridget said putting the boy down in the crib and taking the girl to her other breast.

"Bridget, I don't know what I would do without you?"

"May I say what I feel?"

"Please. There can be nothing that stands between us."

"Come sit beside us and hold my other breast in your hand. I wish to feel you with me again."

Akhu stood and put his fingers beneath her chin and smiled down at them.

"You will be consort and move into the chambers next to mine. I will never marry but you will be my lover."

"To be you lover is my fondest wish."

He kissed her as the baby sucked on her breast.

Bridget returned to his bed after feeding the children in the adjoining room, slipping under a cotton sheet, and laying up close to his sweating body. His hands roamed along her belly already taut and firm after delivering her child.

"That feels wonderful," she said as his fingers played with a round, stiff nipple at the crest of her enormous breasts filling again with milk.

"Was it difficult standing there like a shadow, watching Juji and I as we are now?"

"Yes, it was terribly hard for me, hard to bear. I wanted to be in her place."

"You are now and will be forever, " he said bringing her to him.

As the days passed, Bridget, blooming even more than before, became all of Egypt's symbol of womanhood. She was revered as a wise and close confidant of King Akhu and the protector of the heir who she nursed along with the girl child she named, Alana, guarding and feeding them night and day, never giving them to a wet nurse, always there when they cried for milk.

An artist was summoned by Akhu who posed her in front of a roll of papyrus and painted her image for posterity as the single concubine of the great king, Akhu.

She sat on a small bench, blond hair done in an immaculate coil with gold pins, her blue eyes outlined with kohl, lips with henna, a diaphones panel of silk gauze across her lap, a gorgeous woman. naked and bursting with full breasts above a perfect, oil coated body.

Akhu came often to watch, even making suggestions to the artist about her position and expression.

Half of Alexandria was in love with Bridget but she still wondered about the man who was her king? Akhu, stricken by the loss of his three previous loves, was attentive and kind but she never felt she had his heart.

The Assyrians were restless once again and Akhu, along with a delegation of soldiers and officials, sailed along the coast to their capital for a meeting with the Assyrian king, a meeting Akhu hoped would prevent a costly and dangerous war.

Bridget, as always busy with the children, stayed in Alexandria in the palace. Late one afternoon, her maid announced General Sampson, the young warrior who had been her protector in the battle against the Celts.

Though it was feeding time, she respected his busy schedule and told the maid to show him into her quarters.

General Sampson, wearing a white, Roman style, cotton tunic, came into the room and stopped in front of where she sat nursing the girl child, Alana.

He bowed his head and smiled.

"You have become more beautiful than even the words that have reached my ears," he said.

"Thank you, Sampson. It is good to hear such things when one is confined like this at the end of a sucking mouth for most hours of every day."

Sampson drew a deep breath as he stared at Bridget, naked but for a simple linen loin cloth, the child at her breast half asleep and near the end of her feeding.

"I am amazed that you are so content with all of this?"

"It is what the gods want of me."

"But great beauty should be seen and worshiped by a man."

"Is this why you have come, to compliment me?"

He shifted on his feet and nodded yes.

"And are you not aware that I am King Akhu's concubine?"

"I am sadly aware of that, yes."

"But your eyes tell me something different."

"They have always spoken what I feel, ever since that time we joined our bodies on the ship."

"And you still remember that night?"

"Every second of it."

"You wish to hold me that way again?"

Sampson reddened at the directness of her questions, fear in his heart at what might come of this conversation, a fear he had buried in his great need to see her.

"If only it could be so?" he whispered.

"Come and help me put the child in her crib," she said standing, the child's slack, sleeping mouth still holding onto her nipple.

She walked into her bed chamber with Sampson following and put the baby down in its crib next to the sleeping heir.

"Now, dear Samson. Please realize that I am now Egyptian and follow your customs religiously. Our coupling is allowed by the gods and it is something I wish for. Take me there," she said pointing at a large bed covered with pillows, "and show me how you treat the women you conquer."

He followed as she dropped her loin cloth onto the floor and lay back on her bed.

Akhu returned victorious, having made peace once again with the Assyrians.

"I do not doubt another trip will have to be made soon in order to keep them in line," he said taking off his armor and coming to her bed. "Did all go well in my absence?"

"Yes, Akhu. The children grow like weeds in the delta and I kept busy but anxious for your return."

He smiled and sat on the edge of the bed.

"I have never regretted having only one as concubine instead of a stable of women who are nothing but brood mares."

"You are only too kind and I appreciate your feelings," she said though her mind reeled at what she had done in his absence.

Would he forgive her if he found out? What would he do to her and to Sampson if he discovered she had been with him?

"Come, my King. Let me massage those weary muscles."

An hour later, he rested on her pillows, her head on his chest.

"But, there is something," she said. "Whispers reach my ears that tell of the high priest causing trouble again."

"Will that man never give up? He's not the high priest anymore, nothing but a priest of Osiris."

"He is supposedly spreading rumors to all who will listen that the heir is not the child of the queen."

Akhu sat up.

"Do you fear for the children? I will have him killed at once if you do."

"No. I am safe in your protection and so are they. But, I felt you should know of his intrigues."

"Where did you hear this?" he asked.

"Your General Sampson told me."

Akhu nodded his head and rose from her bed.

"I will speak to him about this."

Summoned by Akhu, General Sampson's brow broke out in sweat. He has found us out, his mind spoke to his heart.

Akhu sat in his chair, rolls of papyrus spread out in front of him as Sampson stood at attention.

"To serve you," he said in the custom of addressing his king.

Akhu looked up then back at a scroll in his hands. Sampson shifted his weight nervously thinking of his punishment, a death worse than any a soldier could encounter in battle.

"What have you done about it?" Akhu asked looking up.

He knows, Sampson thought, perspiration breaking out all over.

"Sir, I only did what my heart demanded."

"What are you talking about, Sampson?"

"It was a mistake and will not happen again."

"What will not happen?"

"Sir, please forgive me. I have learned my lesson."

Akhu shook his head and handed the papyrus to him.

"You are not at fault for this. No one could have imagined the evil of this priest."

Sampson took the scroll in his damp hands.

"You sweat, Sampson. Loosen your neck plate. It is too hot for a formal uniform."

He undid the binding at his neck and let the leather flap fall away. His hands shook as he read but felt some relief when he saw it was a notice by the priest announcing Orsis's displeasure with the boy pharaoh, Cameron.

"What does this mean?" Sampson choked out.

"He spreads rumors that my boy is not the true heir, that the dynasty begun by Sabra has been false from the beginning, and that Egypt must go back to the line of Pharaoh Nebrunef."

"That imbecile man on the throne? I will not hear of it."

"What would you do about the priest and his threats?"

"I would drive a dagger into his black heart."

Akhu nodded.

"Come to our quarters tonight when it is done."

Sampson saluted and left. A killing was far simpler than admitting his guilt.

A maid opened the door and announced General Sampson. Akhu and Bridget sat at a low table eating a small diner, the two children asleep on a pillow by her side.

"I come as ordered," Sampson said while standing at attention.

"Oh, come sit down, general," Bridget said scooting aside to make room.

Sampson pulled a pillow up and sat between them, close enough to her that he felt the heat and smelled the fragrance coming off her oiled body.

"It is done, Sir," Sampson said softly.

"What is done, general?" she asked.

"I asked him to remove the priest from this world," Akhu said. "Let us hope this is the end of his conspiracies."

A maid handed Sampson a cup of beer which he swallowed rapidly, his heart pounding in Bridget's presence, his prayers asking that he not give his passion away.

They ate, Akhu saying little, Bridget talking about the children and the court.

"There are always intrigues at court," she said after a second cup of beer. "Where there are men and women, there will always be secrets."

Samson, again, broke out in a sweat thinking she should not play with words so close to the truth.

"Are there secrets in my court?" Akhu asked.

"I spend my days and nights with the children," she said, "They have little to hide."

"And you, general. Do you have secrets," Akhu asked.

"A general's life is full of secrets and compromises and strategies, else how could he be a good military leader?"

"That is true," Akhu said.

"But you must have some personal ones?" Bridget said, her mouth speaking loosely.

"Ask and I will tell." Samson all but whispered.

"Who do you sleep with at night?" Bridget asked laughing then hiccupped.

"My dear," Akhu said standing and taking her hand. "You must retire. It is not good for your milk to drink strong Egyptian beer."

She got up, smiled at Sampson, and said goodnight.

"Women cannot hold their alcohol like we soldiers, eh Sampson?"

The young general nodded that he agreed, his heart pounding in his chest at the close call. He told himself he would not go to her chambers the following night as they had planned. Somehow, he must break off this passion they shared or they would both die.

Chapter Thirty One - Flight

The Roman Centurion stood before King Akhu in the throne room. They were alone but for soldiers outside the entrance.

"May I approach," the Roman said in a low voice.

Akhu nodded that it was all right to come before him. The Centurion stepped forward where he could speak quietly.

"Sir, we have received a desperate message from my close friend, Augustus, in the Senate. Rome is coming apart at the seams. Our treasury has been depleted, our armies reduced to that of our weakest foe. Rome has been governed badly and there are many who wish to change the leadership."

"This is indeed bad news. Rome's strength is all that keeps the world from falling into chaos."

"As we speak, General Sirius marches with the legions of Rome toward Alexandria. He hates the way Alexandria has overshadowed Rome in power and wealth. He has sworn to right this wrong and marches with his army. We, here, have an almost equal number of legions but, I for one, detest the idea of Romans fighting Romans."

"What can I do to help the Southern Legions who have been at my side in many battles?"

"It is why I have come to you. I do not know what to do?"

Akhu looked at the Roman general wondering if all he said was true yet sensing that it was and that Alexandria and all of Egypt were at risk once more.

"You are well aware that we have been at peace with our neighbors and Egypt's treasury has been spent to build and not destroy," Akhu said. "Our armies are small and no match for a Roman invasion. We will fight at your side but I fear the outcome."

Before the month was over, General Sirius and his legions from Rome appeared on the Sinai desert, ten legions of soldiers from the north to face but seven of the southern province of Alexandria.

The Centurion, reluctant to fight his countrymen, rode out to meet General Sirius under a white flag of truce.

They sat across from each other in the general's tent.

"I have no wish to cause the death of Roman soldiers," the Centurion said.

"You have no choice in the matter. All your men will die as will the Egyptians." the burly, war hardened general said.

"Is there no way to convince you this is a peace loving land and not your enemy?"

The general stood and approached the Centurion, walking around behind where he sat.

"Rome has become a pit of dung. Alexandria is rich and as fair as a good woman. I will have Alexandria and Egypt."

The Centurion sighed and started to stand but fell back into his seat when a dagger entered his heart from behind.

"All is lost, King Akhu," an aid said rushing into his chambers. "They march on Alexandria. The Southern legions have surrendered."

Akhu looked at Bridget.

"Gather the children and Janis. We leave at once."

"Where will we be safe from those traitors?" she said picking Cameron up.

"We ride to the nomads in the desert and the tribe of Juji. We will be safe there. Our lives and that of the heir will be lost if we wait too long. Hurry. Prepare yourself and the children. I must attend to some final things at court."

Under the cover of night, a small procession rode through the gates of Alexandria, Akhu on his black stallion, young Janis at his side, dressed in a Roman skirt and blouse rather than her usual loin cloth. A pair of loyal soldiers rode guard. Behind, in a covered chariot, Bridget rode with the children and a wet nurse.

When they reached the barren Western desert, Janis moved forward, her keen sense of direction honed by a youth growing up like a boy. She led them into the dark night, out onto blowing sand, and away from civilization.

For two nights, she followed the stars west. By day, they rested in shade when they could find it or under the chariot when none was available.

"For a young woman, you are a good soldier," Akhu said as they lay on their backs under the chariot and out of the merciless sun.

She nodded a thank you.

"I will see that you are safe, Janis. Your sister would wish it so."

"I am safe with my king," she said in a soft voice and rolled over to sleep.

"I think that is the most I have ever heard you say but it is true. I will make sure you return to your tribe both well and untouched."

On the fourth night, Janis halted the procession, holding her fingers to her lips for silence. Akhu, on his horse beside her, leaned forward to listen as Janis dismounted, crept to the ridge of a dune and peered cautiously over the top.

Akhu, alarmed, reached for his sword when he saw her stand and whistle into the darkness, Horses hooves vibrated the sand beneath their feet as four mounted nomads raced over the top and came to a stop in front of Janis.

She waved for Akhu to come to the ridge, turned and galloped down the far side toward the nomad encampment.

They sat before the elders. Akhu was warmly welcomed by the tribe as one who had shared their camp with Juji some time ago. Janis sat by his side, quiet, her budding body once again clothed in nothing but a loin cloth.

Akhu explained what had happened, that Juji had died and been placed in her tomb, Only Janis and Bridget knew the truth, that she had died in childbirth only a season ago.

Though saddened by the news, the tribe went on as before, accepting the fate of the gods and the inevitability of death.

A tent was given to Akhu and Bridget where Cameron and Alana were cared for by the wet nurse.

Akhu spent much of his time with the elders yet ventured once to the flat rock where he lay in the sun remembering happier times there with Juji.

Bridget, however, often wandered through the campsite, teasing and tempting all who looked at her magnificent body that was barely covered in the thinnest cloth. She had taken to wearing thick kohl on her eyelids and a deep, red shade of henna on her lips. Fingernails and toenails were painted in gold to match her free flowing hair, something most had never seen on a woman

Though he had long since stopped sharing his bed with her, it worried Akhu that she was making choices that were unbecoming to a King's consort. But there was little he could do to stop her.

Many nights she didn't return to his tent, nights when he sat with the children at the evening meal and held them while they slept.

Bridget stood in front of him, her sweat covered body soiled with sand.

He stared at her with a look of contempt, stared at her disheveled dirty loin cloth, bruises on her arms, and a defiant expression on her once pretty face. He wondered how he had gone so wrong in trusting her, believing she was right for him? What demon god possessed her and opened up this insatiable need that propelled her into the arms of any man? Unable to change her from her promiscuous ways, he ordered an immediate separation of her from the Pharaoh's court. In reward for her services to the crown, she would keep a residence and a small amount of coin when they returned to Alexandria but her visits to his bedchamber were over

"I have announced to the tribal elders that you are no longer my consort. You may stay in my court if you wish but will not share my bed ever again."

"The children? What will you do with them?"

"Are you abandoning the babies as well as your king?"

"I cannot control what the gods have made me. I cannot keep this body from those who desire it. I am merely an instrument of Isis, the fertility goddess."

"You will care for the children as you did before this passion for any man overtook your senses or they will grow up without a mother. Leave my tent and clean yourself up before they wake."

"You speak to me like a king when you are nothing more than a nomad now. I will do as I choose," she said, a desperate expression on her face, then picked up a small sack of coins and stormed out of the tent.

A young man came to the village, half-dead from his desperate trek across the desert from Alexandria, a former nomad but for the last year, a slave in the palace.

"Tell me what you know of my Alexandria," Akhu asked by the night fire after handing him a flask of water.

"It is not as you knew it, sir. The Romans behave like animals. They take whatever they want, the women, a horse if it appeals to them, a coin if it is seen. The city is filthy, not like when you ruled. A person cannot walk the streets without being robbed. The citizens have become as bad as the Romans, and steal what they can. There is no order, nothing but chaos."

Akhu looked at the elders who sat listening.

"It has been a year. I have spoken often about returning to Alexandria. Now, is the time. When the tribes gather for the games by the sea before the journey into the desert, I would speak with them about ending of the misery Rome has spread throughout our land."

The elders nodded their approval, all victims of the cruelty which spread throughout all Egypt, even into the desert.

Five tribes of the western desert gathered for the annual games before they separated to return to their desert homes. Akhu stood before the faces of angry men, the elders of the tribes.

"I have told you my plans. With your warriors and those of the nomads of the upper Nile, we will march on Alexandria and return peace to our land."

Every face in the crowd stared at the king listening to his words. As one they stood and voiced their approval in a loud shout that could be heard for as far as a man could see, one hundred nomad leaders who ruled a thousand men.

"We are small in number but better fighters than the five thousand soldiers that roam the streets of Alexandria, drunk and disorganized. The time is right."

A shout went up again as Akhu smiled at the brave warriors of the desert.

Chapter Thirty Two - Janis

The summer games over, Akhu wandered
down the beach only to find himself standing in
knee deep water by the great mound of boulders. He
dropped his loin cloth to the sand and swam out
through small breaking waves as Juji had taught,
then back to the beach. He stood and looked up at
their flat rock, the place of such peace and where his
love for her began. Realizing that soon he'd risk all
in battle with the Romans, he wound his way
through the familiar crevice, found the hand holds
known only to them, climbed, and stepped out onto
the warm, flat surface of their secret place. As he'd
always done, he lay back, naked and let the warm sun
dry his wet, weary body. His thoughts went to Juji
then to Sabra and further back to Suffi, all women
he'd loved and lost.

Far off and down the beach, he heard the sounds of laughter and squeals of delight from Cameron and Alana who played in the sand with the wet nurse. Bridget was nowhere in sight. Though saddened by his thoughts of those he'd lost, Akhu lay back and closed his eyes thinking of his plans for the battle to come.

"Please do not be angry with me." came the voice of Janis who stood over him.

He shaded his eyes and looked where she stood, the sun silhouetting her from behind and as naked as he was.

"No, it is all right. I was just..."

"May I speak freely?"

"Always. Please do not think of me as your king."

She smiled and lay down beside him, her long, thin body wet from the sea, , damp hair hanging down on young breasts standing high and proud.

"You have become quite the woman, Janis. I hardly believe my eyes."

She turned toward him and said, "You notice little of what is around you such as the way the consort betrays you."

"I am well aware of what she does and she no longer shares my bed."

"That is wise, Akhu."

"But is the freedom she expresses with her actions?" Janis said, "Is that the freedom my sister wished for all Egyptians, where a man and woman couple without feelings for each other? I do not understand."

"Juji did her best to set an example for all. She despised the class system, secrecy, and intrigues of King Nebrunef. She hated the behavior of the eunuchs and priests who set themselves above all others. She lived to change the customs of Egypt that made good and bad marriages permanent, wanted to free people like those in her tribe."

"But the tribe is different. You know this. You were there," Janis said. "We are just nomads, not royals. We have our own customs which are not those of Bridget who embarrasses her king."

"You are very wise, Janis, for someone who is so young. But, don't you see. Though I don't forgive her, what Bridget has done by being with so many men was to expand Juji's freedom even more."

"Yet, it doesn't please you who are pharaoh."

Akhu looked at her innocent face, brow furrowed with concern.

"No, it does not. I am of the old school and find myself only able to care for one woman at a time."

"But you have no one now that Bridget no longer shares your bed."

"That is true," he said looking at the incredible young body of Janis sitting so close that he smelled Juji's aromatic oils on her silky, smooth, olive skin. "That is true. Those words come from my wise, and lovely young friend who sits beside her king and advises him well."

She took his hand and kissed it, saying, "If only I could help you more."

They lay quietly side by side in the sun as he had done with Juji in those wonderful days past.

Who was this little creature called, Janis, this young girl who had been in the background almost constantly since she had joined the court? Though only a few years younger than Juji, she was as pretty and well developed as her sister though as different as night and day. While Juji was fun loving, gregarious, and could talk anyone out of their dearest possession, Janis was serious, quiet to the point of embarrassment, and painfully shy. But something in those qualities appealed to him. Untouched and pure, she quietly ignored the great beauty she had become.

"I am comforted that you allow me to speak freely."

"You were afraid?" he said. "I wish you to be as open with me as with your sister. She would want that to be."

"I miss her."

"As do I."

He looked more closely at Janis lying next to him and said, "You have grown so much in mind and body. I hardly know the young woman beside me."

"Do you remember what you taught me in our little school?"

"Of course."

She stood and faced him, her nakedness outlined in the sun.

"Do you remember this," she said and began to recite a stanza from the Greek poet, Homer.

When she finished, he clapped his hands and said, "You may be the smartest and wisest person in my court, Janis."

She smiled and reached for his hand.

"Let us hope our battle against the Romans is successful," he said letting her pull him up onto his feet. "I would hear more of Homer in our court once Alexandria is free again."

Her face flushed as their bodies brushed against one another when they squeezed through the secret passage, put their loin cloths back on, and walked slowly toward the tribe.

They rode side by side into the desert, almost two thousand armed nomads riding or walking behind them, two thousand men willing to die for their king, the friend of the wandering people.

The lights of night fires in the city brightened the sky that lay within shouting distance from where they hidden in the darkness.

"We will wait for midnight when many will be drunk on our wine and beer and coupling with our women," Akhu said to the officers who stood by his side. "They will not hear or see us coming. In small groups of twenty, fan out all over the city and kill any Roman who resists."

"But, what of the palace?" one of the young men asked. "If it does not fall, we will fail."

Akhu smiled at him and said, "I have fifty men with me and will have the palace before light brightens the sky."

Fifty men, he thought as he sat on his horse watching the sky glow over Alexandria. I would prefer five hundred. Who knows what waits beyond the walls?

A man rode up and told him everyone was in place, two thousand nomads with blood in their eyes.

He gave the order and they moved as one toward the entrance. When just outside, he heard the shouts of drunken men and the screams of women beyond the walls. A house burned unchecked a short distance from the gates.

Arrows flew and the few Roman soldiers on duty fell from the top of the wall. Akhu and his men entered the city and fanned out to their designated objectives.

He led his fifty straight toward the palace killing a few soldiers on the way, drunken men who looked up from their debauchery and quickly fell to nomad swords.

They swept through the gates of the palace and engaged in a fierce fight with a Roman guard then Akhu and ten handpicked men raced through the halls toward the throne room. Janis, at his side, ran as swiftly as the men, a bloody sword in her right hand.

Akhu threw the door to the throne room open and stood before the imbecile king. General Sirius, his face red with anger, held his long sword high in front of him.

"Stand aside, General," Akhu barked.

"Not before you die," the Roman said lunging forward, his blade aimed at Akhu's heart.

Akhu stepped aside and thrust his sword deep into the generals ribcage, the general taking Akhu's blade with him as he fell.

He lay on the stone floor, the sword standing upright from his body, blood leaking out and running toward a nearby drain.

Akhu turned and spoke to the fake king.

"You are not to blame for this. We will see you are well cared for. Please step down and allow me my rightful place on the throne."

The slow witted king wiped his lips with the sleeve of his gilded robe, stood, and sat on the bottom step of the dais, his fingers playing with a loose string on the hem.

Akhu sat as one nomad leader after another reported. Within an hour, the city was quiet and order restored.

Janis stepped forward and bowed her head. Blood ran from a cut on her arm. Her tunic was slashed at the waist, a red welt raised on her belly. Black hair, soaked with perspiration, hung down in front of her wild eyes.

"We have won, Akhu. All nomads salute you, our king and pharaoh," she said still breathing hard.

Many shouts went up from the nomads gathered in the throne room.

"My comrades. I am the one to salute you. Let it be known that the nomads will henceforth pay no taxes and the lands of the open desert are theirs to roam at will with Isis watching over them."

Loud cheers rocked the very walls of the palace as Janis sat on the bottom step, holding her arm where it bled.

He looked at her arm and said, "Men, be sure all who are wounded are cared for. Egypt cannot to afford the loss of one warrior who has fought for her freedom."

A maid ran forward and took Janis to a room where she was bathed and bound with four separate cotton bandages.

The following morning, Akhu stood outside Juji's old chambers and spoke to the maid.

"Is she all right?"

"Her wounds are not serious but she is troubled. I see it in her eyes."

He entered the familiar room to find the young girl in bed, propped up against huge, soft pillows, her long hair down and on her shoulders, a light cotton sheet pulled up to her lap, her bandaged upper body bare but for blood soaked bandages.

"I am told your wounds will heal quickly," he said coming to the side of the bed he knew so well and looked down at her.

"Please, come. I wish for you to sit with me."

Akhu, with the smell of Juji's oils scenting the air around Janis, sat on the edge of her bed.

"You have never looked more beautiful," he whispered. "I hope there will be no scars from your wounds."

"Would it offend you if there were?"

"No. Nothing could mar your beauty."

"Do you mean that , Akhu. Or are you just trying to make a young girl think of other things rather than her king?"

He stared at her, his eyes running up and down the magnificent woman under the sheet who looked up at him with such a serious expression. The body he studied was as fine and perfect as any he had ever seen, a young virgin, destined to make some man crazy for endless nights in the future.

"I have never seen such a gorgeous woman, never," he said in a voice that cracked with emotion.

"But the body you admire has a mind as well, does it not?"

"A mind as sharp as any but, it is your beauty that stuns me. Why have I not seen it before?'

"Men are often blind to what is right in front of their eyes."

He smiled and took her hand but drew it away when she winced from her arm wound.

"No. Take my hand," she whispered. "I have wished for your touch for too long."

Akhu, his heart swelling as it did when he touched Juji, took her hand, felt the warmth and softness as her fingers wrapped around his.

She raised it to her mouth, stared deeply into his eyes, and kissed each finger, long lingering kisses that sent waves of mixed emotions through his mind.

"I feel a great stirring in you," she whispered, "But you must wait."

He looked at her, wanting to crawl beneath the thin, cotton sheet and ravish her body until she begged him to stop.

With eyes wet and soft, she held his fingers to her lips and said, "I wish for it to be perfect when we join our bodies as my king desires. However, it must wait until you can hold me and not my sister in your arms. The time will come."

"But..."

"Go. Think on what I have said. I will lay here and wonder at what you will do to me when your mind is at peace."

He stood and looked down at the most beautiful woman in all Egypt and shook his head in disbelief. No one would dare turn down their pharaoh, their king, but this marvelous creature had done just that. Yet, in his heart, he knew what she had said was true. He could not lay with young Janis and have her sister, Juji, in his arms.

Twice each day for a week, Akhu came to her room and sat on the edge of her bed. Without shame, he stared longingly at her young body, all but bursting out of her oiled, olive toned skin.

They talked for hours on end about every subject known to man but it often came around to those strong men and women who had favored his past, his father, Hepu, One Eye, Suffi, Sabra, Juji, and countless others. She never tired of hearing stories even when he failed to remember he'd already told one to her and repeated it in a slightly different way. He told her of slavery, of battles on land and sea, marches through the desert, and life among those in faraway lands, of kings and past pharaoh's, of court schemes and treacheries.

"For such a young man you have seen a great amount of life and love," she said as he finished telling her of his early days studying in the library with his sister, Sabra.

"I am older than you may think," he said. "As you say, these eyes have seen almost more than one can bear."

She took his hand and squeezed, "To these eyes, you are a good king, a noble and brave king who serves his people justly and kindly."

"A king who wishes to serve you as well," he whispered.

"Be patient, Akhu. Be patient. We have a lifetime ahead of us."

A small bandage on her right breast had come loose and hung down. She reached up to press it back in place but he took her hand away and placed his fingers on it, slowly pulling until it came loose revealing only a red welt where a knife had nicked her during battle.

His finger traced the raised scar and moved down onto soft flesh below, their eyes locked on one another, her hand coming up and covering his. For a long moment his hand held her breast, hers over it, her hand pressing down on his, both breathing hard and staring into the abyss they were falling into.

She took his hand away.

"Please," she whispered. "I am weak, not from my wounds but from desire but I ask you to wait until you have only me in your dreams."

Rattled, Akhu found it hard to speak.

Janis was completely well, all bandages gone, her wounds healed with only a scar on her arm that the surgeons said would be gone in a year.

He stood in the shadows under a library portico and watched as Janis and the children played in the courtyard reflecting pool. All three of them were naked, Cameron racing back and forth swinging a wood sword, yelling and splashing Janis and Alana who sat on the edge of the pool, feet dangling in the shallow water and talking.

Though he loved the children as deeply as any father, his eyes were only on Janis, the fairest treasure in all Egypt. Not one of the Greek or Roman sculptors or painters had captured such beauty in their work. Not one woman in Egypt could compare to her. As he stood and stared at her, he knew what had to be done. Leaving them to their play, he walked to the stable, mounted his horse, and rode out into the desert, a small contingent of soldiers riding by his side.

In the Valley of the Dead, he passed the huge tomb of Pharaoh Nebrunef where Sabra lay then rode to the far end of the valley where a smaller tomb sat alone in the sun and stopped where Juji had been placed for eternity.

With the soldiers waiting, he walked alone to the tomb and stood in front of the slab of stone that sealed her inside.

"I stand before you, my queen, and ask your forgiveness. I have fallen deeply in love with your younger sister but cannot remove you from my mind. Is it guilt I feel? Is it a duty for a king to live in the past? You always knew what was right. What should I do?"

A soft wind blew sand onto his sandals and covered his toes. The silence in the Valley of the Dead was total except for an occasional whinny from the horses or when one stabbed a hoof at the sand.

He stood facing the tomb and wished she could answer.

On one of the staggered steps of the tomb, a lizard crawled out of its hiding place and lay on its belly to take the warmth of the sun. It spread out on the flat, smooth stone and looked down at Akhu with green eyes the color of Juji's.

Startled, he moved toward it, the lizard racing back into its hole in the stone.

"I swear its eyes were the same color as yours and Juji's," he said as they sat on a bench in the courtyard gardens. "It looked at me then darted into a dark crevice as if to say go, leave me in peace."

"It was an omen, a message from her, I am sure."

"But what could it mean?" he asked.

"That is for you to figure out, Akhu. Did you really tell her that you have fallen in love with me?"

"I did and asked her what I should do?"

"What will you do?"

He looked into those bright, green eyes, and smiled.

"No one has been in my dreams but you for as long as I can remember. I will always love her and cannot erase what was in the past. But it is over. I am flesh and blood and so are you. I dream no more of her but only of you. I beg you to believe me."

She smiled and took his hand.

"Let us have another evening where you tell me stories of your Egypt. Come to my rooms. We will sit and I will listen and learn as we have done before. But tonight, I would ask you to remain and not go to your empty bed."

Akhu stood, his feet weak with nervousness, and let her lead him into the palace and her bed chamber where they would have supper, and after his stories, would find relief from the savage desire they both had held in check for so long.

Other books by William Burr are all available on Amazon.com.

Some of his most recent titles are:

Children's Books
The Magic Litter Box, Book One - Atlanta, The City of Glass
The Magic Litter Box, Book Two - Pirates and Treasure
The Magic Litter Box, Book Three - The Water Freighter
Then Magic Litter Box, Book Four - Atlanta, 2013
The Magic Litter Box Collection, Books 1 through 4 - A Space and Time Travel Series

Fiction
Against All Odds, Finnish Ski Troops in WWII
Shattered Lives, Refugees, Smugglers, and Terrorists, a Trilogy
Edge of the World, A Novel of Adventure and Exploration in 1405
Kidnapped by ISIS, One Woman's Battle Against Terror and Corruption
Falcons, A Novel of Uzbekistan Nomads Fighting the Russians
Forgotten, A WWII Novel of Survival on a Greek Island Ignored by the Nazis

Fall From Grace, A Novel of a Jesuit Utopian
Village in Colonial Paraguay

Defying Gravity, A Solar Glider Voyage Around the
World

Mastodon, Two and a Half Million Years in the Ice

Chameleons, Romance in Neutral Switzerland in
WWII

Escape, A World War II Novel of Nazis in Flight
and Avenging Jews

Sabre Jet, A Novel of the Korean War

Rags to Riches, Modern Day Pirates of Somalia

Voyager, Time Travel Journeys Into the Past

1942, Growing Up in Wartime

On the Run, One Woman's Flight from Chilean
Dictator, Pinochet

Island Schooner, Romance in the South Pacific

World War II in New Guinea, A Novel of Native
Rubber Workers Defying the Japanese

Welfare Geese, A Novel of Love, Humor, and
Hunger

Chinchorro Reef, Kidnapped at Sea

Non-Fiction

Retire in Ecuador

Boat Maintenance, The Essential Guide to Cleaning,
Painting and Cosmetics

Stormproof Your Boat, The Complete Guide to
   Battening Down When Storms Threaten

Sailing Tips, 1000 Labor-Saving Ideas

Now and Then, Observations of Our Family

Printed in Great Britain
by Amazon